"Come out on the terrace," he said.

Ronnie followed him past a spacious bedroom, and as she took a few steps forward onto the terrace and looked down at the dizzying view, she suddenly swayed. Red reached out to help her steady herself.

"It's a different sensation, being out here, as opposed to looking out the window," she said apologetically, inhaling deeply. "I'm feeling a little light-headed."

Red steered her inside. He led her into the nearest room and had her sit down. He sat next to her and looked at her closely. "Are you feeling dizzy now?"

She closed her eyes, and when she swayed away from him, Red's arm shot out to stop her. "Okay, take a deep breath," he murmured close to her ear. "Nice and slow. And let it out..."

As she inhaled, her head came up and his lips brushed against her temple, igniting a thudding in his chest.

Ronnie turned her head and opened her eyes at that moment. Those dark chocolate eyes with the soft fluttering of her eyelashes were his undoing.

Dear Reader,

Have you ever dreamed about being rescued by a handsome hero? My heroine, Veronica (Ronnie) Forrester, spins out during a winter storm and is rescued by a tall Irish Canadian. He whisks her away to his Victorian mansion in the picturesque town of Parry Sound, where she has moved to begin a new chapter of her life.

Although Ronnie is not looking for a man, she is drawn to her "Viking" rescuer Redmond Brannigan II. He turns out to be the internationally renowned architect whose firm designed Franklin's Resort, the initiative of her cousin Casson in *Swept Away by the Enigmatic Tycoon*, my first Harlequin book.

Red and Ronnie have both been scorched by their past relationships, but in the enchanting winter backdrop of Red's mansion, where he literally sweeps Ronnie off her feet skating around his Currier & Ives—like pond, the wall around their hearts begins to thaw, leading them toward their happy-ever-after.

Hope their romance warms your heart!

Rosanna xo

Rescued by the Guarded Tycoon

Rosanna Battigelli

Recycling programs
for this product may
not exist in your area.

ISBN-13: 978-1-335-56693-5

Rescued by the Guarded Tycoon

Copyright © 2021 by Rosanna Battigelli

For questions and comments about the quality of this book,
please contact us at CustomerService@Harlequin.com.

Harlequin Enterprises ULC
22 Adelaide St. West, 40th Floor
Toronto, Ontario M5H 4E3, Canada
www.Harlequin.com

Printed in U.S.A.

Rosanna Battigelli loved Harlequin Romance novels as a teenager and dreamed of being a romance writer. For a family trip to Italy when she was fifteen, she packed enough Harlequins to last the month! Rosanna's passion for reading and love of children resulted in a stellar teaching career with four Best Practice Awards. And she also pursued another passion—writing—and has been published in over a dozen anthologies. Since she's retired, her dream of being a Harlequin Romance writer has come true!

Books by Rosanna Battigelli

Harlequin Romance

Swept Away by the Enigmatic Tycoon
Captivated by Her Italian Boss
Caribbean Escape with the Tycoon

Visit the Author Profile page at Harlequin.com.

For my beloved granddaughter Rosalie, who fills my life with joy and laughter. xoxo

Praise for
Rosanna Battigelli

"I was hooked from the first page to the very last one. I fell in love with the characters as I read. The chemistry between them sets the pages alight as you read. I can't wait to read more from this author in the future. Highly recommended author."

—*Goodreads* on *Swept Away by the Enigmatic Tycoon*

CHAPTER ONE

RONNIE'S EYES WERE blinking as fast as the wipers on her car. The fast-falling snow, mingled with the freezing rain pinging against the windshield, was making it hard to focus on the road. Her stomach muscles tightened as she gripped the steering wheel.

She should have checked the weather before heading into town, she berated herself, biting her lip. She had been unpacking boxes from her move to Parry Sound, and oblivious to anything but her task at hand, she had decided to give herself a break and venture out. Her intention had been to treat herself to some books downtown, pick up a pizza and to go back to the cottage at Winter's Haven, where she would spend the rest of the evening relaxing.

It had been snowing when she had started out, but nothing that had caused her to worry. Snow was a given in these parts, sometimes even starting in October. After purchasing the latest Giller Prize–winning novel at Parry Sound Books, Ronnie had continued down the street into Bearly Used Books, a sprawling store with a bear as its mascot. She had floated contentedly in and out of the themed rooms, taking her sweet time searching for a new treasure.

After happily selecting three books—two for herself and one for her son, Andy—Ronnie had proceeded to the front counter. She had vaguely noticed that the number of customers had dwindled, and as she had paid for the books, Melissa, the store owner, had announced that she would be closing shortly because of the freezing rain.

Ronnie had hurried out to her car, her vision blurred by the sleet and gusts of wind. The noticeable drop in temperature would make the ride back to Winter's Haven downright dangerous if the wheels hit black ice on the winding road. She would have to slow right down and pray that other drivers would do the same.

Inside her car, Ronnie wiped her face with some tissues and turned on the ignition. As the car warmed up, she dashed outside to brush the snow off the windshield and windows. She realized how futile it was, though;

she would just have to start driving and keep her wipers going, and hope she could make it back before dark, when the roads would be even more treacherous.

Ronnie breathed a pent-up sigh as she left the downtown, a blur of traffic lights, slick streets and glistening vehicles reflecting the illuminated storefronts. There was no way she'd be able to stop at Maurizio's Pizzeria, she thought, wistfully conjuring up the authentic Sicilian pizzas that her cousin Casson had ordered when she had first arrived a week ago. Her mouth watered at the memory of the spinach and ricotta pizza that she had anticipated enjoying this evening, and then she started as her car swerved as it caught on a patch of ice.

Righting the vehicle, her heart in her mouth, Ronnie slowed down even further.

Concentrate, just concentrate, she kept telling herself, her mouth dry. Her eyes felt itchy from the strain of trying to focus on the road, but she didn't want to lift her hand from the steering wheel to rub them.

Thank goodness her son wasn't with her right now. She would have been twice as terrified if Andy had been in the car with her. Squinting, Ronnie could understand how a person could become totally mesmerized by the hypnotic swish of the wipers as the snow and ice pellets lashed at the windshield.

A sudden beam from a vehicle's headlights jolted her and she shot a glance in her rear-view mirror. An enormous black truck with a massive chrome grille seemed to be approaching fairly quickly. Ronnie frowned. Perhaps the driver wasn't particularly concerned with the road conditions because he or she had studded tires. But even so, he— she was willing to bet the driver was male— should have some consideration for people driving a much smaller vehicle. Especially in this brutal weather...

Ronnie considered putting on her hazard lights and slowly driving off to the shoulder to let the truck go by. She didn't want or need the pressure of driving with an impatient driver behind her. It would be unnerving, to say the least, especially if he decided to pass her. And from the looks of it, he was aiming to do just that.

She would be proactive, she decided. She pressed the hazard lights on, and then veered toward the shoulder. And then it felt like the steering wheel jerked from her grasp and the car was moving of its own volition. It was spinning, she realized numbly. Black ice! Losing all sense of balance and control with the kaleidoscope that was flashing in her eyes, Ronnie closed her eyes and braced herself for the inevitable impact.

She opened her eyes timeless moments later, realizing there hadn't been a life-threatening impact. In fact, there hadn't been a crash at all. Her car had simply skidded onto the shoulder of the road and then come to a stop in the snow-covered field, several yards from the stand of pine trees parallel to the road. Thank God, she thought, her jaw muscles unclenching. She was unhurt but her stomach was coiled in a tight knot, and her heart, which she suspected might have frozen for a few seconds, was now clanging in post-shock alarm.

Blinking, she peered out the window and saw the black truck that had been behind her was slowing down and coming to a stop on the shoulder. Her jaw dropped. "Jerk," she muttered. He could have been going slower, in which case she wouldn't have felt the compulsion to let him drive by.

And she wouldn't be stuck in this mess right now.

She felt her cheeks burn at the thought of what might have happened, how she could have been killed if her car had slammed against a tree trunk. Or an oncoming vehicle. Some angel had been watching out for her.

And Andy...

Ronnie took several deep breaths, trying to calm herself. The worst hadn't happened, thank heavens. She had to concentrate on what she needed to do *now* to get herself and her car back on the road.

She watched as the door of the truck swung open and the driver emerged. Her view was diminished by the icy drizzle accumulating on her windshield, but when she tried to start the car to get the wipers going, the noise her car emitted made her turn off the ignition right away. Muttering an expletive, she waited for the driver to approach. She squinted, catching a glimpse of russet hair before the man whipped the fur-trimmed hood of his parka over his head and started walking toward her vehicle.

He was a giant, well over six feet, and the size of his green parka and jeans-clad legs hinted at broad shoulders and an athletic physique. He took huge strides, but sank with each step into the knee-high snow. Which meant that *she* would be sinking up to her thighs if she ventured out.

Ronnie shivered. Her fingers were starting to feel numb, even with mitts on. The freezing rain pelting down on the hood of the car seemed to have intensified, and she felt her stomach muscles tighten.

She had to call Casson. She hadn't told him or his wife, Justine, that she was heading into town...

She fumbled to get her cell phone from her handbag, and groaned when she saw that the compartment where she usually kept it was empty. It must still be on the kitchen table, where she had absentmindedly placed it before searching for her boots. She was stranded in a town she had just moved to, and the truck driver was getting closer, now just a few giant steps away. She would have to rely on him to help her. The first thing she needed to do was to call her cousin. Then she'd need a tow.

Ronnie took a deep breath, trying to steady her jangled nerves. She was irritated with herself on several counts. First for being oblivious about the weather conditions, and second for skidding off the road, and third for forgetting her phone and being in a position where she had no choice but to depend on a stranger for help. Trust that he meant well...

She had always prided herself on being self-sufficient, but even more so when her husband had decided that he couldn't handle dealing with their son's life-threatening illness and abandoned her and Andy when he was midway through his series of chemo treatments.

The fact that he had found solace with another woman before he left her had been just as hard a blow, and Ronnie had had to wrestle through alternating feelings of shock, sadness, anger, disbelief, resentment and self-pity.

She had struggled, but she had been fiercely determined to carry on, for the sake of their son. Ronnie had vowed to herself that she would never depend on a man again. *For anything.* And now here she was, vulnerable and helpless, with no choice but to depend on this mountain of a man. It was a situation that could have been prevented, she berated herself for the umpteenth time.

Ronnie tapped her fingers against the edge of the steering wheel. They slowed as the man came into view. She could make out his furrowed eyebrows, caught glimpses of startling bluish green in his narrowed gaze, a straight nose and ruddy upper cheeks, and glistening, golden-red scruff that covered his upper lip, well-defined jaw and chin. It matched what she could see of the guy's hair under the hood of his parka. Reluctant to let in the freezing rain, Ronnie waited until the man was a couple of feet away before rolling her window down a few inches. She felt a flutter shimmy down the length of her. He looked like a Viking. A Viking in a Canadian parka.

"Hey there, are you okay?"

His voice was baritone deep, the kind of voice that matched the height and breadth of him, and for a few seconds her words caught in her throat. She was tempted to ream him out for being the cause of her decision to get off the road, which led to her spinout, but conversely, she was grateful he had stopped and had been concerned enough to come to see if she was all right.

Maybe he wasn't a complete jerk…

She stared at him, mesmerized by the crystal clarity of his eyes and the genuine concern in them. "I—I…"

"Did you hit your head?" he asked, leaning toward her. "I don't see any blood from here, but you might have suffered a concussion."

"I—I— No." She blinked up at him.

His frown deepened. "You might be in shock and can't remember. I think it's best if I take you to the hospital immediately. Your car will have to stay here until you can get a tow tomorrow. I doubt anyone would come out now in this weather." He stepped closer to peer in through the opening, surveying her as if he were looking for signs of broken limbs. "Does it hurt anywhere? Your neck? Chest? Legs?"

The warmth of his breath fanned her face. For a moment all she could process was the emerald brilliance of his eyes. And then she heard him asking her again if she was hurt.

"No, no, no." Ronnie shook her head and then winced. "But I have a headache."

"Which is why you need to get checked. You might have hit your head when you spun out, and can't remember, which is common with head trauma… Thank goodness your car didn't flip over," he added huskily. "What did you say your name was?"

"I didn't." Ronnie hesitated. Why would he want to know that? And then it hit her. Of course; he was wondering if she was suffering from a concussion. "Veronica," she said. "Or Ronnie."

"Okay, Veronica or Ronnie. It's not nice to meet you under such circumstances, but it's still nice to meet you. My name is Redmond. Or Red," he said with a smile.

She blinked, and the sudden image of him in a Viking warrior tunic and chain mail ignited a swirl in her stomach. Maybe Erik the Red was one of his ancestors… Ronnie shook her head and met his gaze, her cheeks flaming with the realization that he had noticed her lingering gaze.

"Your eyes look a little glassy," he murmured. "We'd better get you to a hospital and make sure you're okay."

"I—I don't need to go to the hospital. I need to call my—my—"

"Husband," he finished for her. "Of course. But let me get you in my truck and you can call from there. And warm up. I'll have to clear the snow around your tires first, though. And from the looks of it, I may have to carry you over...that is, if you allow me to..."

Ronnie felt her cheeks tingle. Surely she could manage to trudge through the snow on her own.

As soon as Ronnie rolled up the window, he used his gloves to brush off enough snow to allow him to open the door. It made a crunching sound from the built-up ice along its edge. She shifted in her seat to ascertain if she could walk to the truck herself, but realized that the depth of the snow and the quickly darkening sky would make it very difficult. At least there was already a path made by her apparent rescuer.

She had no choice but to trust this stranger. And let him carry her to his truck.

She swiveled in her seat, grabbed her handbag and one of the book bags and hooked them over her right shoulder.

"That'll be an extra freight charge," he said, his tone serious.

Ronnie's jaw dropped. "You've got to be kidding." Her brow furrowed at the teasing look in his eyes. *She* was not in a joking mood.

"Did you actually believe me?" he chuckled.

"Well, I don't know you, so I wouldn't know if you were joking," she returned coolly. "And I'm not in the habit of jumping into a stranger's arms, either." She gestured toward the snow. "But I can see I'd be swimming in the stuff if I don't take you up on your offer, which is really the least you can do."

He looked at her quizzically. "I'm not sure I follow you on the last bit, but you can clarify it in my truck. In case you haven't noticed, I've been getting pelted. I feel like I'm about to become an ice sculpture."

Ronnie's mouth twisted, and she bit back the reply on the tip of her tongue.

"Okay, you can shift your body into my arms and put your arms around my neck. Let me know if anything hurts, all right?"

Ronnie shifted slightly and felt his arms

immediately slide under her legs to support her weight. She managed to click the door lock on the key before she felt him straighten. Her arms instinctively flew out and up to entwine themselves around his neck. As he began taking big strides back toward his truck, she automatically pressed her head against his chest to shield her face from the elements. She closed her eyes and a shiver of relief ran through her. His broad chest was like a protective wall shielding her from the forces of nature. A wall softened by a big warm comforter.

It was an odd feeling, that of being protected. Taken care of...and by a complete stranger. From the crunch of his every step, Ronnie realized that the drop in temperature had caused the top layer of snow to become hardened with the freezing rain. The roads would be like a skating rink. And the country roads would surely be worse.

How would he be able to get her back to Winter's Haven?

Her eyes flew open when he stopped. She felt an unexpected sense of disappointment when he set her down on the shoulder of the road, a couple of feet away from the passenger door of his truck. She shot a glance at the road. Very little traffic, and the cars that were there had all reduced their speed. She eyed his truck. He had left it turned on, so the windows would stay defrosted, and it thrummed like a sleeping monster. Its wheels came up to her waist, but Ronnie still had doubts that it could maneuver its way safely on the winding road toward her cottage.

"I'd ask you to jump in, but after spinning out, you'd better not," he said, his husky voice pulling her back to reality. He opened the door and held his hand out as she stepped up into the truck.

The warmth of the interior blanketed her immediately, and releasing a pent-up sigh, she sank into the passenger seat. Her nose immediately reacted to a familiar scent. *Pizza?* She turned and saw the large box on the back seat with the words *Maurizio's Pizzeria* on it.

The door on the driver side opened and Red quickly settled in behind the wheel. His face broke into a grin. "Hungry?"

Red almost laughed out loud at her expression. It was one of mingled disbelief and something else—like maybe envy...

"I was going to pick up a pizza there," she murmured wistfully. "But I changed my mind when I heard about the freezing rain."

"Well, I don't mind sharing," he said, feigning solemnity. "But first things first. Don't you have to call your husband? And then you can let me know your address. I can either use my GPS or you can tell me where to go." He smiled, turning on the windshield wipers.

"If I wasn't at your mercy right now, I'd probably tell you where to go," she blurted. "Pardon my bluntness, but your monster truck was getting too close for comfort. It made me nervous and I wanted to move onto the shoulder before you zoomed by me and caused an accident." She crossed her arms and tilted her chin defiantly at him.

"Ouch. I left myself wide open for that, didn't I?" He rubbed his jaw. "But let me set the record straight, Veronica or Ronnie. I was approaching because I wanted to let you know that one of your taillights wasn't working." He leaned toward her. "And believe it or not, I was going under the speed limit." He surveyed her flushed cheeks, and eyes which reminded him of chestnuts glistening in the sun. They matched her hair, or what he could see of it under that toque. It looked like she had it up in a ponytail. And her mouth… right now her lips were pursed, but rosebud pink and lovely…

"I forgot my phone. May I use yours, please?"

"Of course," he said, stifling his desire to

chuckle. He found her honesty refreshing. He stretched out to reach into his pocket. "Your hubby must be worried about you."

A frown immediately creased her forehead. She took off her gloves and reached for his cell phone, giving him a clear view of her left hand. *No ring.*

The sound of a male voice was loud and clear. "Hey, buddy, what's up?"

Ronnie looked at the phone as if it were something from outer space and then put it back to her ear. "Hey, when did I become a 'buddy'?"

"Ronnie, is that *you*? And why are you using my friend's phone? Where are you? I didn't know you were out in this weather!"

Red exchanged a confused look with Ronnie. They had a mutual friend?

"Friend?" Ronnie's jaw dropped. "My car spun out and got stuck in a stretch of deep snow off the shoulder. He was behind me on the road and he stopped to help me. I forgot my phone at the cottage."

"Are you all right? Are you hurt?"

"I—I'm okay."

"Are you sure? Let me talk to Red."

Red took the phone. He was curious to find out which one of his friends Ronnie had contacted. And why they had never mentioned this lovely lady sitting next to him now, her chestnut eyes fixed on him with just as much curiosity in their glistening depths.

"Hello? Hold on a sec, I'll put you on speaker. Okay, which one of my 'buddies' are you?"

"Red, it's me, Casson."

"What the—" Red frowned.

"And you've rescued my cousin. Thank God she's safe."

"Cousin?" His gaze flew to Ronnie. Casson *had* mentioned a cousin by the name of Ronnie.

"Are you sure she's okay? She didn't hit her head?"

Red's gaze flew to Ronnie, who was rolling her eyes. "She insists she's fine. There's no sign of bruising. And no bruises on her car, either. Just wheel-deep in snow."

"I'll arrange for a tow tomorrow," Casson said. "As for driving her back to Winter's Haven, I wouldn't advise it. The country roads are iced over. How are they in town?"

"Getting bad. I'll be taking my time getting home."

"Can you put Ronnie up for the night? I'm sure you can find a corner for her in that shack of yours, Red." Casson laughed.

Red chuckled, aware of Ronnie's sudden

scowl. "I suppose I can put up with Ronnie for the night," he said, deliberately switching the words.

"Excuse me, *gentlemen*," Ronnie cut in sharply. "Red can just drop me off at the nearest hotel, if you don't mind."

"Okay, call me when you get there, Ronnie," Casson said. "Thanks, Red. Drive safe."

"Will do. Catch you later."

Red put his cell phone down and turned on the radio, catching the last segment of the sports news. "Weather's next," he said, buckling up. Moments later, they heard the warning to stay off the roads, as the quickly dropping temperature was causing flash freezing and dangerous driving conditions.

Red turned off the radio. "Well, that clinches it," he said, shrugging. "I have no choice but to drive you to my place. The nearest hotel is much farther away." He saw her look of dismay. "Don't worry. It's not that run-down of a shack. Sure, it needs a little TLC, but I'm sure there are worse places to be stuck in…"

"I can't believe this," Ronnie muttered, shaking her head. "What rotten luck."

"It's not *that* bad," Red said consolingly, flashing her a grin. "You get to have some of that awesome pizza. Man, it smells so good.

Let's get outta here…" He rolled down his window to make sure the way was clear. The air was remarkably colder, and the freezing rain lashed at his face. He quickly shut the window. "You buckled up?" Nodding his approval, he slowly veered back onto the road and concentrated fully on driving. Recalling everything Casson might have told him about Ronnie would have to wait until much later…

CHAPTER TWO

RONNIE STARED NUMBLY AHEAD, the wipers swooshing hypnotically left and right. So much for a relaxing evening at the cottage... She was heading to the "shack" of a virtual stranger. The fact that he and Casson were friends was somewhat reassuring, but she didn't relish the thought of spending the night in what sounded like a ramshackle bachelor pad.

At least, she figured, he must be a bachelor. There had been no mention of a wife or girlfriend...

Ronnie stole a glance at Red. He had flipped back the hood of his parka, revealing a shock of hair the color of burnished copper, with curling ends. His jaw and chin had scruff that hadn't seen a trimmer in at least a week. Yet she couldn't deny that he was... kind of cute. Okay, maybe *cute* wasn't the right word for this...this *Viking*.

He turned and caught her staring. She felt heat swooshing up into her cheeks and she blinked, trying to come up with something to say. He smiled, and the heat spiraled back down her body to her limbs. She resisted the temptation to roll the window down to cool her flaming face. "Um, how far is it to your place?" she blurted.

"Can't wait to dig in to the pizza, eh?" he teased, his smile widening into a grin that showed his perfect teeth. He turned his gaze back to the road. "Just a few more minutes before we get to my humble abode—"

The truck suddenly veered to the left and Ronnie cried out, her head swerving against Red as he maneuvered the truck out of the skid. For a few seconds her cheek was pressed tightly against his upper arm, and she closed her eyes, afraid to look. When she felt Red's arm ease up again, she ventured a peek. He was turning off onto a road with no houses in sight, just streetlamps. She righted herself and squinted through the constant swiping of the windshield wipers. Where on earth was he taking her?

Ronnie's heartbeat matched the staccato rhythm of the ice pellets pinging against the truck. And then she caught sight of an ornate Victorian-style gate directly in their path, flanked by sturdy lampposts. Her gaze flew to Red, who had slowed down and was aiming a device toward the gate.

"Open sesame," he ordered dramatically, and Ronnie's eyes widened as the double gate swung open and then closed once they were inside. Moments later an immense three-story Victorian mansion with gables and arches came into view, its bay windows lit up like bright eyes in the dark. A string of lights hanging above a wraparound porch twinkled as they moved with the wind and freezing rain. Red came to a stop in the circular driveway adjacent to the front steps. "Welcome to my 'shack,'" he said, grinning. "I'll get your door."

He put his hood back on and leaped out. He opened the door and put out his hand to help Ronnie down the step, which was already glazed over with ice. "Let's get you in the house, Miss Veronica or Ronnie, and I'll come back for the pizza." He held out his left arm protectively as they went up the half-dozen stairs to the doorway. "I don't want you to slip and get hurt. Your cousin would have my head!" He opened the stained-glass door and motioned for Ronnie to enter.

The foyer was breathtaking, with its carnelian-and-black-tiled floor, creamy white leather high-back chairs and gleaming antique armoires opposite each other that reminded Ronnie of one of her favorite books: *The Lion, the Witch and the Wardrobe* by C. S. Lewis...

"I'll take your coat, Ronnie," Red drawled.

She snapped out of her thoughts and took off her parka, and realized that while she was in Narnia, Red had already hung up his parka in the armoire behind her. She couldn't help noticing the perfect fit of his cable-knit sweater and straight jeans. The forest-green of the former suited him and enhanced the color of his eyes. Now that her boots were off, he was even taller, with a broad chest and defined shoulders that made her wonder if he was a football player... And his hair, ruffled and the color of burnished oak leaves in the fall, had her guessing that his heritage was Irish.

"I'll go and grab the pizza and you can make yourself comfortable in the salon in the meantime." He chuckled. "I guess I shouldn't have hung up my parka..."

She followed Red into a spacious salon with an ornate fireplace flanked by built-in bookshelves that were stocked with some classics as well as some recent titles. Two dark brown leather recliners were positioned side by side opposite the fireplace. An elegant mahogany desk and padded leather chair sat in an illuminated alcove with a large sash window. The curved wall boasted more bookshelves and hundreds of gilded volumes. A couch with a William Morris design and mahogany accents lounged nearby. Ronnie blinked, feeling as if she had entered another century.

Her gaze shifted to the sweeping staircase and upward to the immense vaulted ceiling embossed with roses. She could only imagine what the second floor was like... *And that's where you're probably going to be sleeping tonight*, her inner voice whispered.

"How do you like my new digs?"

Ronnie started. She hadn't even heard him come back in. "Um... It looks like a 'shack' out of a fairy tale," she said dryly. "I was almost expecting Beauty to float down the staircase in her lovely gown, with the Beast right behind her."

Red chuckled. "Well, I can assure you there are no beasts in this place. Unless it's a full moon, and then—" he rubbed his chin and looked at her with narrowed eyes "—my fur grows exponentially."

Ronnie's brows arched and she cleared her throat. How was she supposed to respond to that?

"And I might turn into a beast if I don't satisfy my craving for pizza soon," he said, feigning a growl. "Come on, let's have a bite, then I'll show you to Beauty's quarters." She followed him into a spacious kitchen with a charming hearth and live-edge harvest table, and what looked like brand-new appliances. Red followed her gaze. "I know. You're probably wondering why I ordered pizza when I have a setup like this... Well, I need a break once in a while. I can't cook gourmet meals *every* day of the week."

Ronnie smiled cynically. This Viking friend of Casson's had a joking way about him that she suspected he used to charm the ladies and maybe even distract them from his defects of character. *Which are...?* Her inner voice pressed her for an answer, but she brushed it away.

Ronnie watched as Red pulled off his sweater, revealing a plaid shirt that was now partially untucked. He casually pulled out the rest of the shirt and then went to the sink to wash his hands before getting out some plates and cutlery. He had already set down a bottle of wine and two glasses next to the pizza. "May I?" he said, lifting her glass.

She shook her head. "Just water, please." She sat down at the table.

He complied and then poured himself a glass of wine. "Cheers. We made it home safe and sound."

"To *your* home," Ronnie said. "I'll celebrate when I get to *my* place."

"Speaking of which—" he stroked his chin thoughtfully "—you're staying at Winter's Haven?"

Ronnie had a drink of her water. "For a while," she said casually. She averted her gaze and helped herself to a slice of pizza. She hoped he'd get the hint that she didn't want to talk about her personal life. Instead, she wished she could just blurt out the questions that were piquing her curiosity about *him*. Like what did this guy do for a living? How did he know Casson? Was he from the area? Was he in a relationship? What was he doing in this Victorian mansion?

"I called Casson," he told her before biting into his slice. "He was happy to know that you're safe."

Ronnie nodded and glanced at the leaded casement windows. They could hear the wind driving the freezing rain against the panes. It *was* a relief to be off the roads.

"And *I'll* be happy when you forgive me." He cocked his head at her.

Ronnie stopped midbite and shot him a bewildered look. "Forgive you?" She finished chewing. "Oh, for your part in my spinout? I suppose I have. More or less."

"Aha! I knew it! Some lingering resentment." His green eyes narrowed. "Have you no mercy, woman? I *did* rescue you from the snowy depths of despair and bring you to a safe haven."

Ronnie shook her head in disbelief. Was this guy for real? Perhaps he was an actor for the local theater. He certainly had a flair for the dramatic… She blinked at him, not sure how to respond, and saw his lips twitching.

"Uh…well, I guess I *could* find it in my heart to forgive and move on," she murmured, shifting her gaze to her plate.

"Great—I'll be able to sleep now," he said dryly, reaching for another slice of pizza. "Come on, eat up, Veronica or Ronnie."

She pursed her lips. "Okay, you can choose one or the other. My name, that is," she said pointedly. "Although I generally prefer Ronnie."

"Ronnie it is, then." He nodded, suppressing a smile. She seemed a little tense, but he couldn't blame her, having been spun around in that little car. Thank goodness there hadn't been any oncoming vehicles or sharp rock cuts, like on the highway. Maybe she needed something to relax her. "Since you're not having wine, how about a cup of herbal tea?"

"Thanks, but I think I'll just finish my water, and then, if you would be so kind as to show me to a room…" She pulled back her chair. "And hopefully not a haunted one…"

He chuckled. "The only spirits in this house are in my cabinet over there." He watched her cradle her arms apprehensively. He couldn't help thinking how young she looked, with her hair in a ponytail and wearing a plaid flannel shirt and jeans. He guessed her to be no more than twenty-seven or twenty-eight.

She looked at him intently. "Are you sure? A *mansion* like this must have quite a history. It must be close to a hundred years old." She glanced upward to the decorative tin tile ceiling.

"A hundred and five to be exact. And very well maintained over the years. It's an art designated home."

Red sensed that Ronnie wanted to know more about the place, and maybe even about *him.* "I'll take you for a tour tomorrow, if you'd like," he told her. "I think I'd better get you to bed now."

Her eyebrows lifted and he berated himself silently for his choice of words. The last thing he wanted was to make Ronnie uncomfortable. Or more uncomfortable than she already was. "Okay, Ronnie, let me just pull my big foot out of my mouth, and then I'll take you up to Beauty's suite. Unless—" he cocked his head "—you'd rather stick around and we can twiddle our thumbs by the fireplace."

Her lips twitched. "Sorry. I've got some books I'd like to delve into." She took a couple of steps toward the doorway and then stopped to look back at him. "You'll have to twiddle all by yourself."

Red laughed. "That's no fun. But I will graciously accept your decision, Ronnie. Now let me lead you to a guest room."

A couple of minutes later they were in the hall on the second level, with its original narrow-slat oak flooring and elegant gold-embossed wallpaper. They passed several open doors, revealing fully furnished rooms. He had been lucky to purchase the house with all the antiques and furniture. The elderly previous owner, whose great-grandparents had built the house, had decided to sell when he was told that his condition was terminal. It would make him happy, he had explained to the Realtor, to find someone who would genuinely love and preserve the Victorian home that had been passed down to relatives over the years, since there were no longer any heirs.

Red had been in the right place at the right time. His old university friend, Casson Forrester, had gotten in touch and had hired Red's architectural firm to design Franklin's Resort, a getaway for children who had finished their chemotherapy treatment. They and their parent or parents would be treated to a week at the luxury resort. Red had visited Parry Sound himself, fallen in love with the area, and had decided to invest in a property in the little town known as the "jewel of Georgian Bay's Thirty Thousand Islands" and located inside the UNESCO-designated Georgian Bay Biosphere Reserve.

When he discovered that a Victorian mansion had been listed, Red had immediately made plans to check it out. He would be interested in renovating it, and perhaps designing some unique architectural features for the property. Although his flagship firm was located in Toronto's Harbourfront, with offices in major cities around the world, Red had been charmed by the idea of spending time in picturesque Parry Sound when he needed a break from big-city living. And when he had gone through the house and surveyed the property, complete with a picturesque pond and a stunning view of the channel that fed into Georgian Bay, Red had been hooked.

He had taken possession of it a month earlier, but had only moved in two weeks ago, in plenty of time to settle in and attend the grand opening of Franklin's Resort. He had hired a company to give the interior a fresh cleaning, and the only rooms he had made any changes to were his bedroom and the two guest rooms, with the purchase of new beds and linens, and the washrooms on both levels. He had plenty of time to consider any other modifications. For the next couple of weeks, all he wanted to do was enjoy his new estate and let some design ideas germinate…

"We're almost there," he said, slowing suddenly and turning. Ronnie, whose gaze had been drawn to the open door—and *his* room—across the hall, collided squarely with him. She stumbled backward, dropping her bag of books, and his arms instinctively flew out to grasp her firmly. As her head skimmed his chest, he felt a spike in his pulse. And then she pulled away and his arms dropped to his sides.

"Sorry about that," she said with an embarrassed laugh. She picked up her bag.

"No worries," he said lightly. "But I think we need to practice a little more if we want to perfect our tango for that dancing show on TV…"

Red saw Ronnie begin to frown and then her brow relaxed and she laughed. He was glad she was taking his comment as a joke, and as nothing more suggestive. He stopped farther on in front of a closed door. "This is one of the guest rooms," he said.

He turned on the light switch just inside the door, and gestured for her to enter the room. He felt a tug of satisfaction at the look of wonder and surprise on her face. "I wanted to maintain the Victorian features in most of the place," he said. "This room has just been refreshed—new wallpaper, draperies, linens. In fact, you're the first guest to sleep in the new bed…"

"Wow, I guess I'll know what Queen Victoria felt like," she murmured.

"Enjoy the experience," he said with a half smile. "And make sure to turn on the gas fireplace if you find it cool during the night."

"I'll be fine. I'm always hot at night." She averted her gaze immediately, and Red suspected she was regretting the phrase.

"Okay, then, good night."

She glanced back at him. "Good night," she said, before shutting the door firmly.

Red stood for a few moments, staring at

the door, and then went downstairs to the grand salon. He ambled to the window seat that looked out of the huge bay window onto the channel. The freezing rain hadn't abated; in fact, it had intensified, and Red's view was obscured by the accumulation of ice on the pane.

Even with the limited view, Red felt himself relaxing. He would enjoy visiting this place regularly and experiencing a taste of all the seasons, he thought, inhaling and exhaling deeply. Mr. Cameron Doyle—the previous owner—had wanted to personally meet whomever was interested in buying his mansion, and after chatting an hour with Red over afternoon tea, he had accepted Red's offer, expressing his delight that "a young man of the same Irish heritage" would be purchasing it, with the intention of maintaining it as his family had done for a hundred years.

"And maybe you can find yourself a bonnie lass to marry and have a half-dozen children to liven up the place again." He had slapped Red heartily on the back, and Red and the Realtor had laughed before taking their leave.

Red's smile faded as another memory popped up. The image of his ex-girlfriend, Sofia, whom he had dated for over a year. Red had met her when her family had contacted his firm to redesign an estate and winery they had recently purchased in Italy's Tuscany region. Sofia helped run her Italian Canadian parents' wine business, which encompassed vineyards in Niagara-on-the-Lake, Ontario, and in the Okanagan Valley of British Columbia.

After focusing exclusively on his graduate studies and then his family business, Red had allowed himself to reconsider dating...

It hadn't taken him long to be captivated by Sofia and her little boy, Marco. Red had spent many hours with Marco while Sofia dealt with business calls and regular trips to the family's various wineries. They had agreed to maintain their separate condos, especially since Sofia had a five-year-old son. After she had returned from the ribbon-cutting ceremony at the official reopening of the Tuscany winery, she had dropped a bombshell: she had been seeing the Italian lawyer handling the sale, and she was sorry, but she and Red had been drifting apart in the last little while, and the best thing was to accept it and get on with their lives.

Red remembered blinking at her and thinking: Drifting apart? Yes, she had been spending more time at work, but he had continued to spend time with Marco...

As the weeks went by, Red's initial shock and surprise—even sadness and occasional anger at Sofia's betrayal—had eventually begun to subside. The hardest part was missing Marco. He soon realized that the only genuine love that had existed in the relationship had been that between him and the boy. His sadness over Marco had lingered, but he had realized that he had no choice but to accept the situation and get on with his life.

And he had vowed he would never again get involved with a woman with a child or children.

Not that he didn't want kids one day. And he wanted to experience a close bond with them, something he hadn't had with his own parents.

They had been affectionate and loving when they were home, but as a couple whose award-winning architectural firm had been commissioned to do projects around the world, they had enjoyed extensive traveling and had often left Red in the care of his full-time nanny. They had missed special occasions and milestones in his life, and although his nanny had to be credited with trying to make the events memorable for him, Red had felt the absence of his parents. As he grew older, he became better at masking his hurt and disappointment by pretending to be cheerful and happy-go-lucky.

Red had been popular with the girls in high school—they had liked his easygoing personality and humor—but that facade had threatened to crumble when a date eventually invited him over for dinner. Meeting her parents and witnessing the interactions of a "normal" family would make him a little edgy and he would shift uncomfortably at their probing questions about his family. Despite the impressive meal and their congenial banter, Red would leave with an unsettled feeling in his stomach...and not long afterward, he'd break up with the girl.

Red hadn't realized the true source of his discontent at first. As he continued to date, he'd experience similar feelings of discomfort, followed by a lingering malaise, followed a short time later by him breaking up with the girl. He had always been the one to initiate the breakup. By the end of his final year of high school, the girl who had been his prom date hadn't accepted his excuse for breaking up—the fact that he was studying architecture out of town and it would be too hard for him to keep up with a relationship. "You just want to keep stringing girls along." Sherry had hurled the accusation at him. "You're obviously not the kind to want a serious relationship with anyone, from the look of your track record. Well, go, then!" She had leaped out of his Mustang convertible and slammed the door. "Have a happy life. *Alone!*"

Red had watched her for a moment, a burning feeling of frustration and anger rising into his throat. He stepped hard on the gas and screeched away.

As he drove back to his parents' house—he couldn't call it a home—he had forced himself to take deep breaths in and out. He had parked, strode through the empty house—his parents were in the South of France—and stretched out on his bed to think about what Sherry had said about his track record. There *had been* a pattern. A string of dates…that hadn't lasted.

And it had finally hit him. He had broken off with every date before he could become entrenched in her domestic life. Red had wanted to be a part of his own family, not anyone else's.

Spending time with *them* had emphasized the emptiness in his own familial situation even more.

And he hadn't liked the feeling in his gut…

Red had immersed himself in his studies

at the University of Toronto. Despite the invitations and hints from female classmates, he had stayed clear of relationships. Other than group get-togethers on a Friday night, he had focused on his academic goals.

When he had graduated summa cum laude, his parents had been on the opposite side of the world. Red had paused on the stage during the convocation ceremony, putting on a smile for the commissioned photographer, but his happiness at his achievement had been diminished by their absence. As families had rejoined afterward to take photos and enjoy the reception after the ceremony, Red had instead made his way past his friends and colleagues who were hugging their relatives and quickly returned his robe before driving in his midnight-blue Porsche back to his penthouse condo, both graduation gifts from his parents.

Red had placed his diploma in his desk drawer, opened the sliding doors to his spacious patio and stared at the city lights. Despite all the material comforts he had enjoyed in his youth and the luxury grad gifts, he had felt there was something missing in his life emotionally. He had gone to bed shortly after, telling himself that the position he would be assuming in a couple of weeks' time in his parents' firm would keep him busy, with little time to think about anything else.

Red had focused entirely on the business these past eight years, and his parents had bestowed upon him the role of president when they retired. He had proven his competency, they had told him, and they had every confidence in his ability to continue the Brannigan legacy.

And he had. He was on top of all his firm's ventures. It was just so ironic that when he had finally thought he could seriously commit to a relationship, Sofia had been the one to break it off.

Now, a year since the breakup, Red was excited about his new investment in Parry Sound and the possibilities for the future. He was intent on focusing on his job and leisure time. Alone.

Red left the window seat and headed to his bedroom. He was pleased with the changes he had made to it. A sturdy king-size bed with a slate headboard, extra long, with more of a cottage vibe than a Victorian one. A huge horizontal dresser had been custom-made by a local craftsman, and Red admired its rich grain and live-edge feature every time he entered the room. A sitting area by the bay window featured a pomegranate recliner with a pine-green throw and a coffee table that matched the dresser. The original wood floor gleamed under a Muskoka-themed area rug displaying loons on a lake edged with pine trees.

Under his warm duvet, Red thought about his unexpected guest. The last thing he had expected today was to spend the evening with a lady…and one related to a friend of his. Gazing at his ice-encrusted window, he thought back to what Casson might have told him about Ronnie. He had met with Casson a couple of times during the contractual stages of the project. Red's Toronto team was handling the venture, but Red had taken a few days off to drive to Parry Sound to catch up with his friend from university.

He stretched out his arms and linked his hands behind his neck. He thought back to when he had met up with Casson and his wife and their new baby at Winter's Haven after taking possession of his new house. His brow furrowed as he remembered another person who was there, a little boy Casson had introduced as his nephew… Adam? No, *Andy*.

After Andy had left the room, Casson had told Red about Andy finishing his treatment, and that he'd be one of the first kids to stay at Franklin's Resort when it opened in the New Year. With his mom, Casson's cousin Veronica.

Ronnie.

Red's heart began to pound. And he didn't exactly know why...

CHAPTER THREE

RONNIE LISTENED TO the freezing rain striking her window as she changed into the guest robe she had found hanging in the luxurious en suite bathroom. As soon as she had stepped into the room earlier, she had felt that she was stepping into another century. Her gaze had immediately flown to the elaborate four-poster with its ivory lace-edged canopy panels and plush bedspread with gathered ruffle. A rich Aubusson carpet with floral accents and cream, coral, and light green hues covered much of the polished wood floor. An elegant coral wingback chair and matching ottoman were positioned in one corner by an ornate porcelain fireplace, along with a gleaming coffee table and vintage lamp. On the ceiling, an intricate rose-gold chandelier shimmered with dozens of lights.

After Red had left, Ronnie had checked out the spacious en suite bathroom, a mix of modern and vintage, with its elegant marble and glass features, claw-foot tub and mosaic-tiled shower.

Tightening the belt of the robe around her waist, she padded to the window, shivered at the sight of the freezing rain, and was glad they hadn't ventured any farther. Hopefully, the temperature would rise in the morning, melt the accumulated ice on the roads and Red could drive her back to Winter's Haven...

Red. The name suited him. He was tall and strong. And damn good-looking. An image of the way his broad chest and shoulders had filled out his plaid shirt, and his long legs in jeans, popped into her mind... It reminded Ronnie of a drawing of Paul Bunyan in one of her childhood books. She wondered if anybody called him *Big Red*...

What silly musings, she thought, shaking her head. Why was she even conjuring up such images? She turned off the chandelier and switched on the bedside lamp before shifting the pillows and slipping under the covers. She sighed. The bed was heavenly, and she *did* feel like a queen. She'd have to recount her adventure to Andy when he returned from visiting his father in a few days.

Ronnie's smile faded as she recalled the shock of Andy's diagnosis, their lives instantly changing, the harrowing trips back and forth to the Hospital for Sick Children, Toronto's SickKids, from their home in Gravenhurst, the building tension between her and her husband and the final blow: her husband, Peter, "needing a break" and moving out, leaving Ronnie with the bulk of the responsibility.

He announced months later that he had been seeing a nurse called Meredith, and that she had accepted his proposal to become Mrs. Walsh after his divorce. What had surprised Ronnie the most during this time was that Meredith, to her credit, had encouraged Peter to devote more time to his paternal responsibilities. As a result, Andy was now spending alternating weeks and every second weekend with his dad. And new stepmother.

Ronnie turned off the lamp and listened to the tinkle of ice pellets against the bay window. She felt safe and cocooned under the bedspread. Protected, just like she'd been when Red had carried her to his truck…

Her pulse quickened at the memory of her head pressing against his chest as she tried to shield herself from the slanting freezing rain. A coil of heat spiraled through her, and she brought her palms up to her cheeks. What on earth was happening to her? Surely she wasn't allowing herself to be physically affected by a virtual stranger who had swept her up in his arms for no other reason than to bring her to safety?

Her body was betraying her. Responding to a man's touch—no, to the *memory* of his touch, as if she were starved for a man's caress…

Stop! The last thing she wanted—or needed—was a man's touch. She had come out of a broken marriage. She had continued handling her parental responsibilities independently. Why would she get herself entangled again? And what if—and she prayed it would never happen—Andy got sick again? She couldn't take the chance that whoever she was with would not be capable of sticking it out through the tough—and scary—process of treatment. She wouldn't do that to Andy. Or herself. They had been abandoned once. She would not allow it to happen again.

Ronnie inhaled and exhaled slowly a few times. Her mind knew what it wanted. And didn't want. It was her body that was waffling. Reacting to a tall, strong, dashingly handsome Viking type with Irish eyes and red-gold hair that curled this way and that, and scruff the same color.

So you noticed a hunky guy, her inner voice

whispered nonchalantly in her ear. *It means you're normal. Nothing to get worked up about; it's not like the Viking is out to conquer you...*

Ronnie shivered. She pulled up the covers around her face but couldn't get warm. She considered getting out of bed to look for a blanket but another series of shivers kept her huddled under the sheets.

And then she started at the sudden knock on her door.

"Excuse me for bothering you," came Red's husky voice. "I just wanted to let you know that some power lines have collapsed from the weight of the ice. Electricity's out. And you're on the north side of the house."

Ronnie blinked.

"Ronnie, did you hear me? Are you awake?"

"Yes, I heard you," she called out, sitting up. "Now what do we do?"

"Well," he drawled, "I can see only two options at this point—huddle together under some blankets, or make a roaring fire in the salon..."

Ronnie knew he was joking, but the image of the two of them under a blanket made her pulse jump. She cleared her throat. "I... I'll opt for the fire."

"Right. Okay, then. I'll wait here until

you're ready to come down. My cell phone is charged. I can hand it to you now if you need a light…"

"Sure, thanks." Ronnie managed to find her way to the door without tripping or bumping into anything. She opened the door a few inches and in the bright light of his phone, Ronnie's gaze flew over Red's tousled hair and quirky smile. He had changed into a plaid shirt and a blue-gray cardigan, and in his other hand he held a green cardigan.

"I thought you might appreciate this also," he said. He held out both hands, and Ronnie realized that she'd have to open the door wider. She pulled back to ensure her robe was wrapped snugly around her before doing so. Somewhat subconsciously, she reached for both items. "Thanks," she murmured again and closed the door. "I'll just be a minute."

It was going to be a long night. No power, no heat, and instead of a good night's sleep—which she had just been about to embark on—she would be sitting by the fireplace, trying to keep warm next to a guy she knew next to nothing about, other than the fact that he was a friend of her cousin's and that he obviously made a good living, being able to afford a place like this.

She quickly changed back into her clothes and then glanced at the cardigan. Why not? The chill had already settled into the room, and she imagined the roomy salon downstairs would be even colder until Red got the fire going.

A few moments later, she headed toward the door; then, as an afterthought, she grabbed her bag of books. If the fire was bright enough, she might be able to read a bit, instead of being forced to make awkward conversation with Red.

Ronnie handed the cell phone to him and he nodded, his gaze sweeping over her. She followed him down the winding staircase and into the spacious living area. She was relieved to see a healthy supply of wood stacked in an alcove next to the fireplace. "Oh, good, I won't freeze to death tonight," she said, hugging her arms.

Red paused as he was arranging the logs in the grate to cock his head at her. "I wouldn't let that happen, Miss Ver— *Ronnie*. Casson would have my head." He gazed at her and looked like he was going to add something, but then he gave a rueful smile and concentrated on adding bits of kindling and newspaper to the pile. "Good thing I made sure it was in working order when I bought the place," he said, lighting a long fireplace match.

In minutes the fire was crackling and roaring. Red had turned off his cell phone light, and the illumination was bright enough to read by, but Ronnie sat in one of the high-back recliners flanking the fireplace and just stared at the flames, mesmerized. Her heart twinged at the thought of Andy, and like other times when he was away, she felt like a part of her was missing. A loud crack diverted her attention and she rose in alarm.

Red strode to a nearby window to peer through the ice pellets hitting the pane. "Looks like some branches have snapped off the big oak. The weather's gotten worse. And it's windy as hell. It'll be a nightmare tomorrow..." He returned to sit by the fire. "Well, I don't know about you, Ronnie, but I'm not sleepy at all. How about a glass of wine and we can chat a bit?"

Red had to stifle a smile at the way Ronnie's eyes had expanded at his suggestion. She blinked for a few seconds and then she shrugged. "Sure—why not?"

"Red or white?"

"I prefer white, thanks."

"I won't take it personally." He laughed,

and after a couple of seconds, her frown disappeared and she smirked.

"Okay, Ronnie, I'm leaving you to keep the home fire burning while I take care of your order."

"Um…okay." She looked back at the crackling fire, and for a moment Red sensed a wistfulness in her profile, or maybe even sadness. Was she missing her son? She looked so petite, leaning forward to warm her hands. She had let her ponytail down, and her dark hair now fell to her shoulders. The glow of the flames danced across her features, and Red found himself holding his breath for a moment. Reluctant to let her turn and catch him staring, he turned on his cell phone light and strode to the wine cabinet in the kitchen.

As he gathered a tray, glasses and wine, he thought about the details that had come back to him after Ronnie had gone to the guest room. He had taken a quick shower, changed into a robe and stretched out on his bed, not bothering to pull back the covers. He had returned to the conversation he had had briefly with Casson after Andy had left the room. Casson had expressed his displeasure with Ronnie's husband, who had been unable to cope with the situation, and had gotten his own apartment.

"The poor guy wasn't getting enough attention," Casson had muttered sarcastically. "Well, Ronnie doesn't need a guy like that. She has enough on her plate, dealing with a very sick little boy." He had gone on to say that he loved his cousin and godson and that when Andy had finished his treatment, he was going to suggest to Ronnie that she move to Parry Sound to be closer to him and Justine and the baby they were expecting.

Ronnie had been manager of Casson's hardware store in Gravenhurst, and he would offer her a position as Provincial Marketing Manager, which she could do from any location. She was more than qualified, having graduated with a master's in Business Administration and Marketing, and the bonus was that their kids could grow up together. She needed family to be around her and Andy, Casson had said, emotion catching in his throat. And when Franklin's Resort was built, they would be among the first to stay there for a week's rest and relaxation.

Red had been seeing Sofia at that time, and the news about Andy's illness had made him sad, thinking about how devastated he would feel if Marco were undergoing treatment for a life-threatening illness. Red and Casson had moved on to other points of conversation, but after he had left to drive back to Toronto, Red hadn't been able to stop thinking about Andy. And his mother. Casson had pointed to a picture of both of them from when Andy had turned two. The boy was standing up on a chair at the kitchen table. His little cheeks were puffed up, about to blow out the cake candles, and Ronnie was standing behind his chair, her hands around his waist to ensure he didn't fall. She was beaming at Andy, and Red remembered thinking what a lovely woman she was.

His memory sharpening, he recalled that in the photo her hair was styled in a pixie cut, which suited her heart-shaped face. Now she had let it grow out. Either way, she was a beauty. A wholesome, natural beauty…

Red started as another branch clattered onto the roof. He forced himself to suspend his daydreaming and fixed a plate with a variety of cheeses and crackers. When he returned to the living room, he set down the tray on a small table between the recliners.

He poured the wine and handed Ronnie a glass. "Cheers," he said, grinning. "Might as well make the best of this adventure."

"Cheers," Ronnie said, giving him a curious look as they clinked glasses. "Is your disposition always this cheerful in the midst of environmental adversity?"

He burst out laughing. "Nobody's ever asked me such a question. Hmm." He stroked his jaw. "I generally like to stay positive in adverse environmental conditions and other trying situations," he said. He twirled his glass and met her gaze, amused that she was still looking at him as if he were some incomprehensible species from another planet.

"Are you following some kind of Eastern philosophy or something like that?" she said, genuine curiosity in her voice. "Surely you can't stay positive *all* the time…"

"Well, now, to answer your first question, I do occasionally meditate," he said. "And as for the second, I *have* been known to slip into the dark world of negativity when my hockey team is losing zero to three."

"So you're a hockey fanatic," she said, raising her eyebrows.

"You mean hockey *fan*," he corrected. "Go, Leafs, go!"

"A Toronto fan…" She smiled. "Just like my son."

"Since I was a kid. Forever a faithful fan of the Toronto Maple Leafs." He lifted his glass in a mock toast.

Her lips quirked. "A fan with astounding alliteration ability."

He chuckled. "And you're a lady with a lovely literary lexicon."

She laughed. "Okay, enough. I don't think I can top that." She took a sip of her wine and then set it down as the pelting against the windows intensified. "If this freezing rain keeps up, you'll have your own skating rink in your driveway."

Red saw her brows knit together. "Are you worried about your son?" he said gently.

Her gaze flew to his. "How do you…? Of course. Casson told you about Andy…"

She looked at him with narrowed eyes, almost as if she were speculating how much he knew about her personal life.

"No, I'm not worried about *him*. At the moment, that is." She glanced at her watch. "By now, he's been fed, bathed, read to and tucked into bed." She shifted her gaze to the fire for a few moments and then suddenly turned toward Red again. "Do *you* have any kids?"

Red's eyebrows went up. Ronnie was treading in sensitive waters. The relationship that he and Marco had shared had felt close to a father-son relationship. In fact, they had done what most dads seemed to do with their kids: play sports and games, go to the park, read, help with homework, go fishing... The thought that he wasn't doing any of those activities anymore struck him hard. *Again.*

A year may have passed since the breakup with Sofia, but his feelings about Marco hadn't dulled or changed. He missed the lad. *A lot.* And he vowed to himself every night that he would never cause himself this kind of grief again... Realizing that Ronnie was waiting for him to respond, he shook his head. "No, I don't have any children," he said with feigned lightness. "Or a wife."

Something flickered in Ronnie's eyes... Was she curious whether or not he was seeing anybody? "Or significant other," he added with a twist of his lips. "You know the saying—once burned, twice shy. To be more accurate, I've been scorched..."

Ronnie's eyebrows tilted slightly. "Sorry to hear that," she murmured, and turned to gaze into the fire.

"And yourself?" He might as well ask, since she had delved into *his* personal life.

She turned swiftly to face him again. "I went through a few flames myself," she said, lifting her chin. "Things have cooled down though, and I intend to keep it that way..."

"So does that mean you're with somebody but are giving him the cold shoulder?" he said wryly. "Or are you freezing out any and all would-be suitors?"

She frowned, then laughed curtly. "They're not exactly knocking at my door."

"Their loss," he heard himself say, and watched as a coral flush bloomed on Ronnie's cheeks.

"My gain." She shrugged nonchalantly. "Andy is my main focus, and his welfare and happiness are all that matter to me. I don't want—or need—any distractions from people who look like men but who are really needy little boys that can't cope when your attention strays from them..." She shifted and looked as if the cardigan she was wearing was making her itch. *Ouch.* He could almost envision the protective enclosure around Ronnie. With barbed wire on top...

"Casson had mentioned something about you moving to Parry Sound..." he said casually while placing another log in the fire. "So you're staying at Winter's Haven?"

"For now." Ronnie nodded. "I want to take my time looking around before I buy a house. I'll probably wait until spring. After all the snow is gone." She fixed him with a curious stare. "So what made you buy *this* place? It's rather large for just one person…"

"It is, isn't it? I'm looking forward to designing some new features and redesigning other areas. This is an art designated home, or 'heritage home,' so there are laws as to what can or can't be done. I just moved in two weeks ago. And I plan to entertain eventually—that is, if I can manage to make any friends," he said, chuckling. "I'd like to hold old-fashioned garden parties in the summer, skating parties on the pond in the winter—"

"There's a pond?" There was a note of awe in her voice.

He nodded. "Like something out of Currier & Ives."

"So you bought this place because…?" She gestured around her.

"First, because I have this thing about Victorian homes. When I was a kid, I always thought they looked enchanting, with their turrets and gables. I imagined all sorts of secret rooms and underground tunnels that led to caves in the hillside. I wanted to build a house like that when I grew up. And second, because I fell in love with the area when I first came to visit Casson after he got in touch with my firm in Toronto."

"Your firm?" Ronnie's brow furrowed mo-

mentarily before her eyes widened. "Do—
do you mean the firm that designed—" She
broke off, emotion catching in her throat.

"Franklin's Resort," he finished. "And I'm
looking forward to the grand opening…"

CHAPTER FOUR

RONNIE REALIZED HER mouth was gaping. She closed it promptly and tried to process what Red just told her. Discovering that her rescuer's architectural firm had been the one chosen to fulfill Casson's dream—and that he would be at the grand opening... It was all too much. "So you're Red Brannigan...of Brannigan Architects International..." she said wonderingly.

"The one and only," he chuckled. "Actually, that's not true. I'm named after my father, so I'm officially Redmond Brannigan II. But since everyone called him Redmond, I became Red. And to tell you the truth, I much prefer it. Redmond sounds kind of stuffy, don't you think?"

Ronnie just shrugged, at a loss for words.

"Although 'Red' and my glorious mop of hair did leave me open to some childhood teasing," he said, his mouth twitching. "I remember that during an art lesson in grade three, a new kid in my class called Ivan started teasing me about my hair when the teacher was distracted. He called me 'Carrottop Four-Eyes'—not the most original of insults—and then crossed the line when he added, 'Your mom and dad must be ugly carrottops too.'" Red's eyes glinted with amusement. "He hurt my feelings, of course, and I did what my inner warrior instinctively told me to do: I dipped my paintbrush in my jar of orange paint and managed to give his blond hair some nice highlights." He laughed, shaking his head.

Ronnie couldn't help but burst out laughing. "That must have landed you in hot water."

"Indeed." He grinned, showing perfect teeth. "We were both sent to the principal's office immediately. But seeing the look on everyone's faces in the class—some of them had been insulted by Ivan the bully, as well—made it all worth it. In fact, I think I remember our teacher trying to hide a smile. I have a feeling that she and others might have been glad that he had gotten his just deserts."

"Did he plan his revenge?"

"Actually, he left me alone after that. Which is what bullies often do when you stand up to them. Not that I condone what I did," he added wryly.

Ronnie pictured Red as an eight-year-old with his russet hair and glasses, and couldn't help smiling. He must have been a cute kid… and an adorable baby, with a head of soft, reddish brown curls…

"What are you smiling about?" He fixed her with a piercing gaze.

Ronnie hesitated for a moment. "I was imagining you as an eight-year-old. And as a baby." She let out a chuckle. "I'm sure you were cute back then."

His eyebrows lifted. "Are you implying I'm no longer cute?"

Ronnie felt her cheeks begin to ignite. "I I didn't mean… I mean, I wasn't… I—"

"Okay, sorry, Ronnie." He leaned toward her, grinning. "I didn't mean to put you on the spot. I don't expect you to comment on my current state of cuteness or lack thereof."

The heat in Ronnie's cheeks intensified. The crackling of the fire seemed to synchronize with the sparks dancing along her nerve endings. With the darkness around them, with only the light of the flames illuminating them both, it felt as if she and Red were in the spotlight like two actors in a play, his body so close that his energy was palpable. He was looking at her squarely, his leprechaun eyes glinting mischievously from only about a foot away, the firelight flickering over the strong lines of his face. He was close enough for her to reach out and run her fingers through his—

She blinked and cleared her throat. "Well, I wouldn't exactly call you Ugly Carrottop Four-Eyes," she replied lightly. "I only see two eyes…"

"I'll take that as a compliment." He smiled. "How about you? I mean, were *you* teased as a child? I can't imagine that you had anything to be teased about…"

His eyes swept over her so quickly that Ronnie wondered if she had imagined it…

"Well, actually I was," she said, drawing herself up in the recliner. "Some kids tried to torment me with a couple of names: 'Shortie' or 'Rabbit.'" She tilted her chin defensively. "But I didn't care. I liked rabbits." She took another sip of her wine.

"So we have something in common," he said softly. "You were the rabbit and I was the carrottop." He continued to gaze at her intently, and then gave his head a slight shake as if to redirect his thoughts. "I've never met a rabbit that *wasn't* cute…"

Ronnie felt her pulse quicken. Was this his enigmatic way of saying that he found her cute? Did she want him to find her cute? "Um, well, I'm sure Beatrix Potter would agree with you," she stated matter-of-factly. "I just wish I could hop home…"

"What? I may not be as cute as a bunny, but I didn't think my company or conversation were *that* bad…" His lips drooped into a pout and he blinked dramatically.

She couldn't help but laugh. "Now you look more like a sad puppy dog." *Still cute, though. More than just cute…*

Red burst out laughing. He held up his wineglass. "Let's toast to bunnies and puppies, the cutest little creatures in the world."

She held up her glass and realized in embarrassment that there was barely a mouthful left.

"May I?" Red reached for the bottle.

"Ah, no, thanks, I'd better not." She leaned toward the fire to glance at her watch. "I think it's going to be a long night…" She shifted in her recliner. "I feel like I'm on a night flight on an airplane. I doubt I'll be getting much sleep tonight…"

"The recliner does recline," he said. "Here, just press on this." He stood up and leaned over to indicate the hidden button. "And keep your finger on it until it's as far back as you want it to go."

Ronnie's pulse quickened as his arm brushed hers and she caught a whiff of his cologne, an exotic spicy scent. When she pressed on the spot, the recliner glided back. She felt self-conscious with Red towering over her while her body moved back with the chair.

"Try to catch some sleep," he said huskily before throwing another log onto the grate. "I intend to do the same." He strode over to a couch on the other side of the room and came back with a thick scarlet throw. "This should keep you warm, especially if I fall asleep and the fire burns out." He smiled, unfolding the throw and placing it over the length of her body. "Good night, Ronnie."

Something fluttered in her chest as Red looked down at her, his face reflecting the shifting light of the fire. "Good night." She closed her eyes until she heard his recliner slide back. She stole a sideways glance at him and saw that he had stretched out without a throw, and his arms were crossed over his chest.

And he was looking right at her.

Red smiled and turned his head away from her. He certainly didn't want to make Ronnie feel uncomfortable. He imagined it was already awkward enough for her, being stranded in a stranger's house in the middle of an ice storm. Well, at least knowing that he and Casson were friends would have eased her mind somewhat.

He listened to the crackle of the fire. The room had warmed up, especially around their recliners. Outside, the freezing rain was still pelting the windows, intermittent gusts of wind making it sound intense.

He had absolutely no inclination toward sleeping. How could he, with a woman he didn't want to be attracted to lying not three feet away from him? She was easy to look at, with her dark hair and dark almond-shaped eyes. He had never seen lashes that long, and he was pretty sure they weren't fake. She was petite, but Red had sensed her inner strength even before he discovered she was Casson's cousin. The cousin with the little boy who had undergone treatment for leukemia. He felt a surge of empathy for what they must have both gone through. It had been hard enough for Casson...especially after having lived through the experience with his younger brother. And losing him.

Red was glad Casson had thought of him and his firm when contemplating his dream of building a resort in Franklin's memory. It had led him to reconnect with his university friend in the picturesque town of Parry

Sound and eventually invest in the Victorian home he had always dreamed of but never got around to building himself. He traveled extensively around the world, keeping abreast of the many projects being developed by his firm's international branches, and when he had visited Casson, he had realized that he needed a place where he could truly take a break from business and just enjoy a more relaxed lifestyle.

Scenic Georgian Bay and the Muskokas had hooked Red immediately. As his pilot had flown Red's private plane to Parry Sound in the middle of autumn, Red had been mesmerized by the forests ablaze with brilliant hues of red, orange and yellow. And now that he had moved in, he was taking a month off for the simple pleasure of making this house a home.

And now, he couldn't deny that he was attracted to Ronnie.

And he was fighting it.

She wasn't free. Whatever fates had decided to slide her into that field and send him trudging through knee-deep snow to rescue her, had just complicated his life. He had thought that after getting over Sofia, and reconciling himself to the sad fact that his relationship with Marco was over, as well, he would be immune to another relationship if it involved a child. He had been adamant that it would never happen again. He couldn't take the thought of building a relationship with a girlfriend's child, only to have to deal with the acute grief of having it come to an end. He had vowed over and over again that any future relationship would happen only if the woman were free. *Childless.*

So even if his body *was* physically attracted to Ronnie, his mind would not allow him to encourage any emotional attraction. He had had to ignore the spike of his pulse when he had lifted her and carried her to his truck, the thud of his heart when she had huddled against him, the empathy that had stirred in his chest at the thought of what she had had to endure, and the pleasure of laughing with her...

Red shifted in his recliner. It *was* going to be a long night. He closed his eyes. His thoughts flitted back to the moment he had seen the vehicle in front of him begin to skid. His heart had jolted, and he had immediately slowed down, hoping the driver wouldn't careen into him. He had been more worried about the impact on the smaller vehicle than on his considerably larger truck. And not for the vehicle itself, but for the passenger or passengers inside. Were there children in the car? Elderly folk?

He had watched it spin out and stop, still upright, off the shoulder and in a field, its tires buried in deep snow. It had all happened in mere seconds. And in a matter of seconds he had maneuvered his truck safely onto the shoulder, leaped out, and trudged through the snow to make sure the driver and any passengers were okay. He'd call 911 if he had to, although with the icy conditions it would certainly take longer for an emergency vehicle to get there safely.

He had proceeded to the car with his head down to avoid the sleet, his heart thumping erratically. Through the partially glazed windshield, the female driver sitting with her hands on the wheel had looked dazed but unhurt. But he had needed to make sure…

Discovering Ronnie's connection with Casson had surprised him, but the memory of some of the details about her and her son had jolted him. It was one thing to have had Casson tell him about his remarkable cousin who was tiny but tough, a real "mama bear," dealing with her son's illness and treatment, but to be with her in person was even more revelatory. He could sense her determination and desire to be independent.

Despite the fact that she had allowed him to carry her back to his truck, he had no doubt that she would have trudged through thigh-deep snow herself had he not stopped to check on her.

Red closed his eyes. He wondered if Ronnie was asleep or awake and thinking like him. And if she was doing the latter, who was she thinking about? Her son? Probably. Him? Probably not.

He couldn't hear the sound of her breathing with the crackling of the fire. After what he felt was a reasonable amount of time, Red turned in his recliner to glance over at Ronnie. Good. Fast asleep. "Sweet dreams," he whispered.

She had pulled the blanket up to her chin, and gazing at her small outline and the way her long lashes rested on her heart-shaped face, Red felt a surge of protectiveness.

And contentment, knowing she was safe.

He inhaled and exhaled deeply, and allowed himself to drift off, hoping his dreams would be just as sweet...

CHAPTER FIVE

THE TANTALIZING SMELL of food cooking woke Ronnie up. Disoriented, her eyes opened to take in an unfamiliar ceiling, an unfamiliar room and a crackling fire. A turn of her head revealed an empty recliner. And then awareness returned.

She was in the home of Red Brannigan, her Viking rescuer…

From the amount of light in the room, she figured it must be midmorning. She couldn't believe she had managed to sleep that long. Or even that she had fallen asleep so quickly. After turning to find Red's gaze fixed on her, she had felt a shiver running through her. He had given her a casual smile before turning the opposite way, no doubt having sensed how awkward she had felt. She had turned the other way herself, and closing her eyes, had wondered how she could possibly fall asleep with the vision of those intense blue-green eyes imprinted in her memory.

She had pulled up the blanket, feeling somewhat vulnerable. Not because she felt frightened in any way; knowing that Red was a friend of Casson's was enough to reassure her of Red's character. Rather, it was more of a feeling of suddenly being aware of a few uncontrollable physical reactions she was experiencing in Red's proximity. And not wanting him to know it. It was silly, really. How could he possibly know how his presence—his height, his strength, the way his russet hair looked after he ran his fingers through it, his crystal-clear Viking eyes—was affecting her?

Her body was a traitor. She didn't *want* to be attracted to Red. She didn't *need* that kind of distraction in her life. Her life was full. More than full. Her responsibilities as a mother were her top priority. She had no business investing any of her thoughts in any man right now.

You have nothing to worry about, she told herself. Red would be driving her back to Winter's Haven, and there wouldn't be any reason for their paths to cross again, other than at the grand opening of Franklin's Resort.

His husky laugh nearby startled her. "Hey, do I have to cook *and* bring you breakfast in bed?" Red was standing in the doorway, a whisk in one hand. His hair was damp, and he had changed into a pair of black jeans and a teal pullover.

Eye candy.

She felt a rush of heat at the unbidden thought and hastily brought the recliner up, realizing she must have undone her ponytail during the night. She smoothed her hair down self-consciously and shot back, "I didn't expect or ask you to cook. I expected only a ride back to Winter's Haven. But since the power has been restored and you have gone to the trouble, I will help consume your culinary creation."

He burst out laughing. "Oh, no. We're not starting the day with literary linguistics, are we?"

"Actually, I prefer to start my day with a strong cup of coffee. And then another. Hopefully coffee's on?" she said, tilting her chin imperiously.

His mouth quirked. "It's waiting for me to pour it in a cup for you, *Miss Veronica*. And I'll be waiting to serve you in the kitchen." Flashing her a grin, he gave a bow, turned and disappeared into the next room.

Ronnie smirked. He seemed to enjoy flinging teasing remarks at her. Well, she would fling them right back at him, at least up until the time he drove her back to her cottage. She folded the blanket and placed it back on the recliner along with the cardigan Red had given her, before striding to the nearest window, anxious to see the aftermath of yesterday's freezing rain and snow. Her hope that she'd be able to get back to Winter's Haven sometime that morning plummeted. At some point during the night, the freezing rain had solidified with the considerable drop in temperature. The limbs and branches of the oaks and maples flanking the driveway were encased in ice. The sky was clear, and the bright sun made the trees glisten as if bejeweled. The snow that had remained on the ground was coated with an icy sheen, as was Red's truck.

Ronnie didn't need to hear the weather report to know that she wouldn't be leaving anytime soon. It might be different in town and on the main roads, where the sand trucks had probably already passed over, but this place was obviously not in a high-priority area, being situated on the outskirts…

She took a deep breath and let it out in an exasperated puff. Along with being a little stiff from sleeping on a recliner all night, she felt out of her comfort zone. And she didn't like it.

Although she hadn't been that long at her Winter's Haven cottage, she had felt at home right away. Casson and Justine had had it refreshed with new furniture and linens, and some homey touches. They could stay in the cottage as long as they wanted, Casson and Justine had reassured her. And, her cousin had added with a wink, she and Andy could babysit A.J. when he and Justine needed a date night... Ronnie couldn't help smiling at the thought of Amy Jay. She was an absolute doll, with Casson's dark brown hair and Justine's blue-gray eyes.

Ronnie turned away from the window. Like it or not, she had no choice but to spend the next few hours in a stranger's home. The last thing she had envisioned when she had left the cottage yesterday was being stranded in a Victorian house with a Viking type who seemed to take everything in his stride. What on earth would they do while waiting for Mother Nature and the town crews to make driving possible?

She would have breakfast and then find herself a spot where she could bury her nose in one of her newly purchased books. And, like it or not, she'd have to be patient. With any luck, she'd be back at Winter's Haven sometime in the afternoon...

A wave of longing washed over Ronnie. She wished Andy was with her, at the cottage, sipping hot chocolate and doing a jigsaw puzzle together, or making peanut butter cookies, his favorite. She gave her head a shake. She should be glad—and she *was*—that Andy's father was taking responsibility and regularly spending time with him. But even so, there were moments where she missed Andy's presence. Many moments...

Casson had given her a reassuring hug when she had voiced these feelings to him one day over coffee. "You may be small," he had chuckled, "but you're still the protective mama bear. You've always put Andy first. He's been the center of your world. Of course it feels strange now to be on your own for blocks of time without him..."

Ronnie sighed and made her way to the kitchen. To her embarrassment, her stomach gave a loud grumble as she entered the room.

Red's eyebrows lifted. "I guess I'd better feed you before there's an aftershock," he chuckled. He gestured for her to sit down at the sturdy oak table, where he had arranged two place settings, two mugs and a carafe. He filled Ronnie's mug. "Enjoy," he said. "I'll be back with the breakfast special." He winked conspiratorially. "And then, since the roads are still a skating rink, we can talk about what we want to do…"

Red watched as Ronnie took her first bites of the mushroom and cheese omelet and nodded when she gave him a thumbs-up.

"Whew! Thank goodness I passed *one* test, anyway…"

Ronnie's brows furrowed. "And what is the other test for? Doing a good deed of the day?" She took a sip of her steaming coffee. "I believe rescuing a stranded driver *does* fall in that category."

He grinned and gestured at his head. "My halo should be lighting up any minute. So—" he gazed at her "—since we are housebound for the moment, we might as well have some fun…"

Ronnie's fork paused in midair. She stared at him as if he had suggested something wild and inappropriate.

"I don't need to be entertained," she said stiffly, her expression wary. "I'll be quite content reading one of my books." She lowered her gaze, concentrating on cutting her omelet into small, precise pieces.

Red gazed at her thoughtfully. She wasn't

going to allow herself to relax. She had just given him the not so subtle hint that she didn't need his company while stuck in his house. A sudden thought occurred to him. She hadn't had a lot of time for "fun" while dealing with her son's illness and treatment these last couple of years. She had probably forgotten what having fun was...

"Hey, I could bury myself in one of my books, too," he said lightly. He had stocked the built-in bookshelves on either side of the fireplace with several boxes of his own books as well as a dozen from his recent trip to the local bookstores. "But why not live a little?"

He watched her as she dabbed at her lips with her napkin, avoiding his gaze.

"You can tell me to mind my own business if you want, Ronnie, but I think maybe you've had to put life on hold while caring for your son—"

"Andy is my life," she blurted defensively. "He's my priority and always will be."

Red felt a twinge in his stomach at her words. "You're obviously a good mother. A very good mother," he said softly. "Andy's lucky to have such a devoted—and strong—parent."

Ronnie's eyes flickered. "I *had* to be strong. I had no other choice."

"Everyone has a choice," he said, unable to keep a hint of bitterness out of his voice. "My parents chose to prance around the world on business and pleasure. That was *their* priority. I guess they figured their only son would have no problem growing up mostly with a nanny…"

She frowned. "I'm sorry…"

"Don't be," he said bluntly. "Thank goodness I was healthy and they didn't have to spoil their plans to come back and take care of me. Besides, I had a great nanny."

"I… I…that's too bad." She shrugged and shook her head. "The first part, I mean."

"It could have been worse," he said, making his voice sound cheerier. "I never lacked for food, clothes, or money. In fact, I shouldn't really complain. It's not everyone who ends up with a Porsche and a fancy condo as grad gifts."

Her brows lifted and she blinked at him. "Yes, but—"

"Let's not talk about me," he said firmly, reaching for his cell phone. He texted something, waited, then looked back at Ronnie. "Just what I suspected," he said, rubbing his chin.

"What do you mean?"

"You said you had no other choice. Well, you didn't, not with a name like Veronica."

"I don't get it."

"I just looked up the meaning of your name. It says here 'Veronica—she who brings victory…and true image.'" He turned off his phone. "Well, it obviously takes a strong person to bring victory…and everything you've done to support your son has helped to bring that about." He felt his gaze soften as her eyes misted. "Andy's in remission. Don't underestimate *your* part in his recovery, Ronnie."

"I did what I had to do," she said, her voice wavering slightly. "My hus—*ex*-husband couldn't handle it. He left, and found comfort crying on the shoulder of another woman. And eventually moved in with her." She inhaled deeply and exhaled slowly. "I took a leave from work. I had to travel back and forth to Toronto's SickKids, watch my little boy subjected to treatment that left him weak and vulnerable. It was—" she bit her lip "—heartbreaking. And then for months, Andy couldn't leave the hospital, and so I ended up staying at Ronald McDonald House. It was…tough."

Red felt a surge of anger inflaming his gut. He could only imagine the emotional ordeal she had experienced, having her husband take off, unable to cope. Coping had fallen completely on *her* shoulders. His gaze took in the decisive tilt of Ronnie's chin as she speared a piece of her omelet. His anger gave way to admiration. Despite her petite size, she exuded an air of inner strength and determination. She had carried on without her deadbeat of a husband.

Well, at least the guy had smartened up and had resumed his parental responsibilities. And if Ronnie had chosen to forgive him and move on, Casson had told Red, then *he* would have to, as well. At least now, Ronnie could have some time of her own. Time to enjoy life— especially since Andy was in remission—and have some fun.

Red dug into his omelet. The weather report earlier had indicated that the temperature was warming up. The crews were still out sanding the side roads. By sometime in the afternoon, driving should be able to resume all over town.

So they had about three and a half hours left in each other's company. And as much as he loved to read, he had other plans. The challenge was getting the determined woman sitting across from him to consider what he had in mind.

Ronnie looked up suddenly and met his gaze. She swallowed and set down her fork. "Thanks, it was good," she said. "A treat not to have to make my own breakfast," she added with a soft laugh.

Red felt a warmth radiate in his chest. She deserved to be treated. "Glad you enjoyed it," he said casually. "I'll treat you to lunch if the roads aren't cleared by then."

She smiled, but Red could tell she was uncomfortable at the prospect. She stood and tucked her chair back in. "Since you cooked, I'll be glad to do my part and wash the dishes."

"Not a chance," he laughed. "The dishwasher will take care of that. But—" he stood up and crossed his arms "—I'm hoping you will accept my challenge to change your plan to read since that can be done any time and come outside with me instead…"

"Outside?" Her gaze flew to the window. "For…what?"

"Let's just say, I'd like you to experience the magic of this place. The conditions are perfect, with last night's freezing rain…" He gave her a warm smile. "Trust me, it'll be a lot of fun…" At her look of suspicion, he chuckled. "If you don't enjoy yourself, I'll give you your money back."

Ronnie gave him a measured glance. "I don't know what I'm getting myself into, but I hope you have good insurance."

He burst out laughing. "Come on, Ronnie," he cajoled, "grab your coat and mitts. You won't regret this."

Moments later, carrying her boots in one hand, Ronnie followed Red past a series of rooms to a hallway that led to the back porch. The sun was streaming through the decorative leaded windows, dotting the wall with prisms of light. Ronnie sat on the long upholstered bench and, still mystified, began to put on a boot.

"You won't actually need those," Red said. "Because—" he opened the doors to an antique armoire and gestured to the contents "—we're going skating!" He grinned. "I invited Justine and Casson over last week. I suggested they leave their skates here for the next time."

Ronnie's jaw dropped. She told Red that *she* had babysat A.J. with Andy last week. Casson had told her they would be out skating, but A.J. had started to fuss and he and Justine had been too busy trying to settle the baby down to give any further details. As soon as she had settled, they had hurried out the door, reassuring Ronnie that they'd be home in a couple of hours. And when they did return, Ronnie didn't linger, as Andy had complained of a headache, and she wanted to get back to the cottage so he could rest in his own bed.

She looked at Red and at the skates and then back at Red. "But I... I haven't skated in years. Besides, I doubt Justine's skates will fit..."

"Justine has small feet. Try them out." He handed her the pair of white skates that were comfortably broken in. His pulse skipped a beat as her hand brushed his. The fact that Ronnie had agreed to go outside instead of reading, as she had originally intended, pleased him. A lot.

He took out his own pair and sat down next to Ronnie to put them on. As he was lacing up his right skate, he glanced up at her. "Well, Cinderella? Does the shoe—I mean skate—fit?"

"Wow; I can't believe it," she said. "We actually take the same size."

"Fabulous. Lace 'em up, and in the meantime, I'll go check the surface of the ice." He finished lacing up his left skate and then gave her an appraising glance. "When you're ready, just come on out." His lips twitched. "You can't miss the quasi-Olympic-size pond."

"That's what I'm afraid of," she retorted, "when I face-plant."

"I'll be on standby," he assured her. "I'll scoop you up before you do..." And with a wide smile, he went out.

CHAPTER SIX

SHE WATCHED HIM through the windows. He was impossibly tall, and he strode toward the pond. Her gaze went from the blue-and-white Toronto Maple Leafs toque on his head to his wool-lined denim jacket and jeans, and finally to his black skates. When he had sat next to her, leaning over to tie them up, she had almost laughed at the sight of her diminutive pair next to his. But when his thigh had momentarily pressed against hers, the amusement she had felt changed to a pulse-quickening sensation that left her immobile. And then he had made the Cinderella comment, and she had responded casually, although inside she had felt a tingle go through her...

Satisfied that her laces were tied snugly, Ronnie stood up, testing her balance on the plank flooring. She proceeded cautiously to the door. She had been a decent skater in her youth and teenage years, and even in the early years of her marriage to Peter, but after Andy was born, skating had not been a priority. And when she had contemplated introducing Andy to the national sport, he had been diagnosed with leukemia.

She sighed. It had been heartbreaking, seeing how restricted Andy's life had been for the last couple of years. While other children were enjoying all the traditional activities of childhood, Andy was undergoing his chemotherapy. She had spent countless hours at his bedside at SickKids, reading to him, singing, and dreaming of the day when he would be able to go home and be a kid again.

Those dreams had come true. She was filled with gratitude every day for the success of his treatment, and she prayed that he would continue to get stronger. And eventually catch up with his friends.

And now that they were settling into Winter's Haven for the next few months, she could even contemplate getting Andy a pair of skates and taking him to the arena...

She smiled, mentally conceding that it was a good thing that Red had gently pressured her to do this. If she was going to take Andy out on a skating rink, then she'd better brush up on her skating skills.

Knowing that the property included a

pond and actually seeing it were two different things. Ronnie paused in the doorway, momentarily stunned. Who had a pond this size in their backyard? The previous night's freezing rain had turned it into a giant, polished mirror. Squinting from the glare of the sun's reflection on the ice, she diverted her gaze to the current owner of the place. *Redmond Brannigan II.*

He was skating around the perimeter of the pond, and when he caught sight of her, he sped toward her in long, confident strides, coming to a dramatic sideways stop, the edge of his skates skimming off the top layer of ice.

"Don't expect any Ice Capades maneuvers from *me*," she declared, stepping gingerly onto the ice. "I don't do any of that fancy stuff."

"I'm not expecting anything other than you having fun," he said. "Just enjoy." He flashed her a smile. "I forgot to do something," he said enigmatically. "I'll just be a moment."

He went back inside, and for a few seconds Ronnie stared at the huge expanse of ice before her. A swirl of anticipation ran through her. Who wouldn't want to have this entire pond to themselves? She started off slowly, reacquainting herself with the feel of the ice and the rush of cool air on her cheeks as she picked up some momentum. She felt like she was in another world, the sun dazzling her and turning the ice surface into a sparkly glass lake. She breathed in the crystal cool air as she began her second lap, her strides more confident. For a moment she tilted her face to the sun, daring to close her eyes. She felt bold, free and an exhilaration she hadn't felt in years. Her heart racing, she opened her eyes, and, with a jolt, realized that Red was at the porch door, watching her.

As he stepped out and approached the pond, a popular rock song came on out of nowhere. When he was near enough to Ronnie, Red pointed to the speakers on posts around the pond. "They obviously enjoyed their skating parties here," he said. "I thought you might enjoy a little musical interlude while we skate."

Ronnie had slowed down, but the beat of the song was catchy and made her want to keep skating. She nodded and zipped past Red as he flashed her a Cheshire cat grin. Her heart flipped. Was she dreaming, or had he just said, "That's my girl?" She shook her head, her heart pounding in synch with the bass, and berated herself for even thinking such a thing. The movement compromised her balance and she felt the edge of her right skate wobbling and lifting off the ice. And then she was falling. Backward...

She closed her eyes, bracing for the fall. But instead of landing hard on the ice, she felt herself being swooped upward. Her eyes flew open and all they could register at first was the sight of the boards whizzing by.

And then it hit her. She was in Red's arms as he skated around the pond.

"I told you I'd scoop you up if you fell..." he murmured in her ear without stopping.

Ronnie was speechless. The sensation of being carried—no, *swept away*—in Red Brannigan's arms was heady. He held her in strong arms, his long strides never faltering as he skated around the pond. Like the day before when he had carried her effortlessly to his truck, she found herself leaning against his broad chest.

Was he going faster? He was. Her arms flew up and involuntarily encircled his neck, her hands clasped together. He suddenly veered toward the center of the pond and as he circled in a figure eight, Ronnie couldn't help letting out a high-pitched yelp. She closed her eyes, convinced he would take a misstep that would send them both tumbling down. Her heart was drumming so hard, she could barely hear the music. She felt terrified and excited at the same time. At the next swirl, she felt her cheek pressed against Red's neck and she couldn't pull away from the centrifugal force.

His neck was warm, and the sensation took her breath away. Her lips were close enough to—

She gasped as he spun her around in a dizzying on-the-spot rotation, forcing her to shut her eyes again, and when he finally stopped, a few seconds passed before she tentatively opened them. He was looking down at her, his sun-flecked eyes glittering above a crooked smile that she could only describe as impish. No, *devilish*. And then he set her down slowly, her hands unclasping and falling limply at her sides. He kept a steadying hand under her left elbow, and she couldn't help but feel relieved, not knowing if her feet would hold her up after that…

"I can't believe you did that," she said breathlessly. "I should be mad at you for scaring me half to death…" She paused at the unapologetic twinkle in his eyes. How could she be mad, though, when the last few minutes had been nothing short of exciting? Unbelievably exciting, activating sensations throughout her that she had never felt before… "I suppose I should just be grateful," she said, feigning a scowl, "that you didn't toss me up in the air and then attempt to catch me…"

He threw back his head and laughed. "Maybe next time," he said huskily. "But seriously, Ronnie, I hope you can forgive me for my impetuous skating maneuvers." He gazed down at her, his hand still under her elbow, despite the fact that she felt steady on her feet. "I just wanted you to have a little fun…especially after the stress of yesterday…"

There was a warmth in the depth of his eyes that Ronnie knew she wasn't imagining. They were the color of a tropical lagoon…inviting and startlingly beautiful.

And sexy, an inner voice whispered.

His eyebrows lifted, and with a jolt she realized that he was waiting for her reply, not reading her thoughts.

"I do," she blurted. "Forgive you."

His mouth curved into a smile. "Great, now let's seal it with a…"

Her heart stopped.

"…hot chocolate. *And,* since you've been such a good sport," he added, a twinkle in his eyes, "I'll add some marshmallows on top."

Red placed the steaming mugs of hot chocolate on a tray and brought it to the living room. Ronnie had replied to Casson's text on Red's phone, and was standing by the window, a wistful look on her face.

She walked over to the recliner she had slept on the day before. He set the tray on the side table between the recliners and sat down. "I checked the weather report, Ronnie. The roads are much better in most places. I'll be able to drive you back to Winter's Haven whenever you're ready."

She nodded and took a sip of her hot chocolate. "Nice," she murmured. "I can taste the cinnamon and something different in here. Nutmeg or cloves, maybe?"

He gazed at her pensively. Her tone was pleasant, but he sensed that something was off. She seemed more subdued…maybe even a little sad…

She took another sip, and when she looked across at him, her brows tilted as she waited for his reply; he couldn't help smiling at the puff of melting marshmallow on the tip of her nose.

She cocked her head at him, and he felt something undeniably sweet tingling through him.

Something dangerous…

Yet some other force made him lean toward her, his hand ready to—

And then she became aware of the white puff and wiped it off herself with a nearby tissue.

He leaned back again, not sure if he felt relief or regret. He took a sip of his hot chocolate and wondered what she was going to do once she got back to Winter's Haven.

"What are your plans today?" he said casually. "Will your son be back?"

Her head shot up, and the look she gave him made him realize that he had ventured into private territory, territory that she was very protective of...

Of course. She was the mama bear, and naturally, she would be vigilant over her little one. And of their privacy, as well. "Sorry, I didn't mean to be nosy," he said gently.

Her features relaxed. "It's all right. For a moment I forgot about your connection to Casson and that he had told you about Andy..."

And about his remarkable mother. "Yes, and what a brave little boy he is..."

Ronnie's eyes misted. Damn, he didn't mean to make her emotional. He opened his mouth to apologize, but she put up a hand.

"I'll be okay." She sighed. "There are days when I can think or talk about what he's been through and not fall apart." She pressed her fingertips against her closed eyelids for a moment. "And then the slightest words or memory will—" Her words caught in her throat, and she looked at him and shook her head. "It's been hard. Really hard." She swallowed. "On both of us. And scary, worrying every day about the future..." She shook her head. "No, it hasn't just been hard. It's been hell..." A few tears slid down her cheeks.

"Falling apart is okay, Ronnie," he said gently. He wanted to reach out, wipe her tears, put a comforting arm around her, but something held him back. "It's good to get your feelings out. That's part of the healing process." He gave a slight grimace. "I'm sorry. You've probably heard this all before."

"I have," she said, nodding. "But it doesn't hurt to hear it again." She inhaled and exhaled deeply. "It's amazing what some people say to you, though, like 'You have to be strong.' If I had a dollar for every time that was said to me..." She bit her lip. "I know people were just trying to help. It's just that sometimes hearing those words really got to me. I *knew* I had to be strong. Nobody had to tell me." She traced a finger over the rim of her mug several times while her forehead creased. Red wondered what memories she was revisiting.

Suddenly she set down the mug, her gaze riveting back to Red. "But to answer your question, Andy won't be back from his dad's until the end of the week. So my plans are to keep unpacking—not everything, though, since I'll be looking for my own place in the spring. How about you?"

"Me? I'll probably continue working on some of my renovation ideas. This place is in great shape, but I'd like to make a few changes, if I can. Maybe replace some of the wallpaper. Since it's a heritage home, there are laws as to what can or can't be done."

Ronnie nodded. "There must be a lot of fascinating nooks and crannies in a place like this." She looked around appreciatively.

"I'd be happy to show you around," Red offered.

"Thanks, but I think we should head out," she said. "I really have a lot to do still."

"No problem," he said, rising. "Maybe another time," he added impulsively. "And—" He stopped himself. What was he doing? He had almost said "And bring Andy too."

He shouldn't have even suggested that there might be "another time" to Ronnie. Much as he had enjoyed her company—maybe too much, especially when she was in his arms— he had to remember that she had a child. A sweet little boy. And that's why he had to stay away. Or make sure *they* stayed away. He couldn't risk getting to know another boy who wasn't his. And although he probably couldn't avoid them at the opening of Franklin's Resort, there was no reason why he would be seeking Ronnie's company otherwise…

She was looking at him, waiting for him to finish his sentence. "And…good luck with your unpacking," he said brusquely.

Moments later, as he drove out of his neighborhood, Red sensed a different dynamic between them. He and Ronnie had been in each other's company for less than twenty-four hours, and yet he found himself experiencing the anticipatory awkwardness of saying goodbye.

Was she feeling something similar? She had been subdued since getting into his truck. But then again, she was probably missing her son.

He turned on the radio. Might as well liven up the atmosphere… He switched a few channels, and settled on the classic rock channel. He couldn't help singing along to some of the catchy tunes, and several times, he caught Ronnie's amused glances in his direction. When one of his favorite songs came on,

"Small Town" by John Cougar Mellencamp, he got through the entire song, and at the final harmonica segment, he whistled along.

As Red turned into the winding road on the final stretch to Winter's Haven, Ronnie gave him directions to her cottage. He slowed down even more, conscious of the intermittent patches of ice on the path flanked by trees. A final turn brought him to cottage number three. Ronnie's car was sitting in the driveway and she clapped when she saw it.

"Casson deserves a batch of cookies for this," she said, grinning.

"He's quite a guy." Red smiled back. He parked behind it and turned off the ignition. "So if *he* gets cookies for arranging a tow, what do *I* get for my heroic rescue? Not to mention my culinary effort and the outdoor entertainment I provided?" He batted his eyelashes as he looked at her pointedly. "I think I deserve at least a cookie or two. Or maybe twenty…"

Ronnie burst out laughing. "If I had my phone, I would have taken a video of you. I'm sure it would have gone viral."

"Really? Well, here's my phone. Let's give them something to talk about…" He sang the last phrase. He pulled off his toque and ran his fingers through his hair, making it stick out, before batting his lashes at her again.

"I'm going to pass," she said, holding up a hand. "Besides, I don't think that performance would do anything for your image as the owner of Brannigan Architects International."

"Fine!" He patted down his hair. "But don't get distracted from the fact that you offered to make me a couple of dozen cookies."

"What?" She looked at him with an exaggerated frown. "Casson should have warned me about you…" She opened the side door and glanced back at him. "But I do offer you my thanks and appreciation for your aforementioned heroism and associated efforts."

She walked gingerly up the steps to her door, then turned and waved, a slight smirk on her face.

He rolled down his window and waved back. "Peanut butter cookies are my favorite," he shouted. Grinning, he backed up before driving off slowly, conscious of Ronnie watching him until he turned and disappeared from view.

CHAPTER SEVEN

RONNIE SHOOK HER HEAD and unlocked her door. She took off her coat and boots and put on her fleece-lined slippers. Feeling a little cold, she turned up the heat and then sat down on the couch, covering her legs with the checkered throw. She gazed at the dozens of boxes that still needed to be unpacked and sighed. It was a task that needed to get done, but somehow, she had no desire to get to it right now. Or anything else. Except maybe baking a batch of cookies for Casson later in the afternoon.

There was no way Red had been serious about baking him cookies, as well…

Peanut butter cookies, his favorite. Just like Andy.

He had been in a joking mood; he was just teasing her…

Or maybe not, her inner voice suggested.

Ronnie frowned. She wouldn't think about

it for now. She'd rather read. She glanced at the doorway for her bag of books. Confused, she wondered in dismay if she had left it in Red's truck. And then she realized she hadn't remembered to take the bag with her. It was on the floor next to the recliner she had slept on.

Damn. Now she'd have to make arrangements to get it from Red. A thought occurred to her. Maybe Casson was planning to meet him before the grand opening, and if so, Red could give it to him.

Her cell phone suddenly rang, and she jumped up to get it on the kitchen counter where she had forgotten it. It was Casson. He had seen Red's truck go by. He asked if she was okay, and if she wanted to drop over for lunch.

"Thanks, Cass. Yes, I'm fine, and thanks too, for getting the car towed. Um, I'll pass on lunch… I had a big breakfast, so I'll just munch on something a little later, but I will drop by this afternoon, okay?"

After hanging up, Ronnie stretched out on the couch and gazed out the huge living room window that looked out onto the water. It had started to snow again, and as she watched the flakes tumbling gently down, she was glad she had some time to herself. She felt bad about declining Casson's invitation, but she needed to process everything that had happened since her car had spun out of control. It was true what she had said about breakfast, but she couldn't exactly tell Casson that this architect buddy of his had spun *her* around. Literally and figuratively.

And much as she loved Casson, Justine and the baby, Ronnie knew that she'd have little A.J. in her arms immediately if she went over. She would delay that pleasure until the afternoon, once she had baked the cookies.

Okay, start processing, her inner voice urged. *Start with his looks.*

Ronnie closed her eyes. She could see him approaching in long, purposeful strides, assaulted by the freezing rain. His dampened russet hair and piercing blue-green eyes. The strength in his arms as he carried her to his truck. His broad chest in that teal pullover and perfectly fitting black jeans today. She had had no problem with the way he looked…

What about his personality?

He was positive, creative, attentive, daring, funny, a good listener, empathetic, silly, charming…

What are his negative qualities?

Ronnie frowned. She tried to think of

something Red had said or done that had irked her.

His teasing? Mmm…no, she hadn't minded it; in fact, it had made her feel a swirl of different emotions, but none of them were bad.

What he *had* done was make her feel something that had been missing in her life since Andy had become seriously ill. The feeling of being lighthearted. *Alive.* When Red had swooped her up, preventing her from falling on the ice, and then skated around the pond with her in his arms, she had felt like a switch had been turned on inside her.

She could keep the truth from Red, but she couldn't keep it from herself. Red had turned her on. Made her remember that she was a woman. And that life was fun.

She had lost her sense of play, of adventure, of joy. Of course she had felt joy at the success of Andy's treatments, but all the other emotions before that—worry, fear, despair, loneliness, sadness—had weighed her down. Peter taking off had made her cynical. Cynical about men, about ever putting her trust in any of them.

And she had been determined *never* to allow herself to get involved in another relationship. She wouldn't risk it. She had Andy to think about. She couldn't put him through that. His little heart had had enough to deal with…

And *her* heart had been bruised enough.

Ronnie took a deep breath and strode into the kitchen. She and Andy would have a good life in Parry Sound, and enjoy being close to Casson and his family. They would share seasonal traditions and celebrate their children's milestones together. She was so looking forward to this new chapter in their lives…

Ronnie began gathering the ingredients for the peanut butter cookies. For the past year, she had been adamant that she didn't need or want a man in her life. So why, then, did she now feel her resolve suddenly wavering?

Ronnie glanced out the window, her gaze dropping to Red's tire tracks on the snow-packed driveway.

You have Red Brannigan II to blame for that, an inner voice replied.

Red's grin lasted for about a minute after leaving Ronnie's cottage until he realized he had done what he had vowed not to do. Suggested a way for him to see Ronnie again. Over cookies, for heaven's sake. Although Ronnie hadn't really taken him seriously. How could she, after he had made it a point to act like a clown?

He liked to joke around, that was part of his personality, and his business associates and employees appreciated his easygoing attitude, but what exactly had he been trying to accomplish with Ronnie? Yes, she had been amused, and just seeing her lose her preoccupied expression and laugh outright had sent a tingling pleasure through him.

Nevertheless, his words and actions were going against his vow not to become interested in a woman with a child. And getting involved with Ronnie and Andy could be even more problematic than any relationship he had had with Sofia and Marco.

Marco had been healthy. Under no restrictions or limitations. Time spent with him had been carefree, with no worries about the child's immune system being compromised. And Marco's mom had been even more carefree, having no problem leaving him under Red's care while she conducted business out of town or even out of the country. Getting closer to Ronnie and her little boy would not be a carefree situation. They had both suffered a huge ordeal in their lives. Emotionally and physically. Andy was in remission, but that didn't mean there were no conditions that they still had to be mindful of.

So what was pulling him toward Ronnie's

sphere? What had he been thinking about, offering to give her—and almost inviting her son— a tour around his mansion? Had he taken leave of his senses?

When exactly had his plan backfired?

He *was* interested.

His brain was swirling with so many emotions. Desire. Desire to stay away. The instinct to protect and the instinct to withdraw. Didn't he have enough on his plate, being the president and owner of one of the most prestigious architectural firms in Canada and around the world?

He had to go back to the house and think about this. Deep down, it worried him. Worried him because being with Ronnie had felt good. *Really good.* He had enjoyed being with her, listening to her share her story, her feelings. He had felt a surge of excitement sweeping her up and skating around with her in his arms. It had been a heart-racing, exhilarating experience, and he was almost sure that she had felt the same way. He had liked the way she had clasped her hands around his neck, with her body pressed against his.

His imagination began to wander...

He gave his head a shake. He needed to concentrate on the road, not fantasize about how it would feel for him and Ronnie to be pressed against each other in different circumstances...

A few minutes later he pulled into his driveway. Inside, he strode into the grand salon, got the fire going and then decided to make himself a strong, dark coffee to clear his mind.

He sat on the recliner that Ronnie had used and, sipping his coffee, spotted a bag on the floor nearby.

Ronnie's book bag.

His pulse spiked. Now he would *have* to see her again. He doubted that she would drive all the way to his place to get them back. He set down his mug and picked up the bag. He withdrew the books and smiled at the first one, *Decorating Your Country Cottage with Nature's Gifts.* He lifted it to see what her second selection had been. *Adventures with Hercules the Hamster.* He flipped through the pages, chuckling at some of the illustrations. Andy would have fun with this one.

Red stared at the title of another book: *Moving On: Embracing a New Chapter of Your Life.* He flipped the book over to read the blurb on the back cover.

You've chosen this book because of circumstances in your life that have either forced or compelled you to move on. A separation or divorce, perhaps, or the loss of a loved one. The end of a job or a friendship.

Whatever life challenges or ordeal you have faced, this book will help you to move forward physically, mentally and emotionally, and to embrace this new chapter in your life.

He opened the book and scanned the table of contents.

Chapter One: Accepting the Past.
Chapter Two: Looking at Your Options.
Chapter Three: Packing Up and Moving Out.
Chapter Four: Becoming the Author of your New Life.

And so on...

Red pictured Ronnie flipping through its pages in the bookstore, her gaze resting on the chapter titles. Had she accepted the past? Was she looking at her options? She had packed up and moved out of her previous town, so maybe she'd skip that chapter.

Red turned to chapter one. Had *he* totally accepted his past? With a cynical twist of his lips, he started reading...

Disoriented, Red realized he had fallen asleep. The book was resting on his chest, pages down. He closed the book. The intermittent sleep he had had the night before—ensuring the fire didn't die out, and due to his inability to stop thinking about the dark-haired beauty an arm's length away—had caught up to him, and he had nodded off on the third page.

He checked the time on his cell phone. Really? He couldn't believe it was midafternoon. In a few hours it would be dark. He should really head out to Winter's Haven now. He didn't have Ronnie's cell number, so he couldn't text her to let her know he'd be dropping off her bag of books. By now she would have realized she had forgotten them. She didn't have his number either, but Casson did. Yet she had not thought to get it from her cousin. Or maybe she just didn't want to...

Red strode to the washroom and splashed some cool water over his face. He examined his reflection in the mirror. His scruff could do with a trim. He could do that himself now. And maybe he'd go for a haircut tomorrow, before driving back to Toronto midweek for an important meeting with his team and a prospective client. He put on his parka and boots, pressed a code into his phone to ac-tivate a set of intermittent lights inside and left, bracing himself against the cold wind.

Hopefully Ronnie would give him a warmer reception…

CHAPTER EIGHT

RONNIE GAVE AMY JAY a gentle kiss on the forehead and handed her back to Justine. She had been quite content sitting in her high chair and playing with her while the adults had their cup of coffee and some of the peanut butter cookies Ronnie had brought over.

She had put some in a tin for Casson and Justine, and some in another tin for when Andy returned. Somehow, there was still a dozen left over.

Red's request had popped into her mind. Or maybe it had always been there.

With a flutter in her chest, Ronnie had left the extra cookies on the tray and had walked over to Casson and Justine's to fill them in on her rescue by Red.

There were some details she had chosen to keep to herself… Feelings that had sprung up from out of nowhere, that were too new, too private to share. How could she possibly tell Casson and Justine that something crazy and magical had happened out on the pond with Red? Something she still needed to make sense of…

It had started with the feeling of freedom as she skated around the pond, a feeling that somehow had been buried under all the responsibilities she had had to manage over the last few years. And then that feeling had catapulted to a whole new level when Red had literally swept her off her feet.

Casson's questioning look drew her back to the present.

"So what did you think of Redmond Brannigan II?" Casson said after Justine had left the room with the baby.

The sudden question made her start. "Um… well," she said, shrugging, "he… I thought he was decent enough to stop and see if I needed help…especially since…"

Casson's cell phone buzzed. His eyebrows lifted and his gaze flitted back to Ronnie before he texted back and then put his phone away.

"By the way, Cass, I forgot a bag with some books at Red's place." She paused, thinking how "at Red's place" sounded so…*familiar*. "If you're in the area, could you maybe stop and pick it up?"

Casson finished his cookie. "No, I can't, sorry."

She stared at him blankly.

His eyes crinkled in amusement. "I can't because Red just texted me. He said he was around the corner and was going to go to your place to drop off something you had forgotten, and then stop by here to discuss some business, if I was free. I texted him that you were at my place. He'll be here any minute."

Red pulled into the driveway. His headlights shone into the kitchen, and he could see Casson and Ronnie looking out toward his truck. There was a look of surprise—or was it shock?—on Ronnie's face.

He shut off his lights and ignition, grabbed the bag and made his way to the door. "Long time no see," he said, a corner of his mouth tilting upward as the door opened. "Hi, Ronnie."

"Hi." She looked down at the bag he was holding. "Sorry you had to come out all this way to bring these back…"

"I'm not sorry," he said, handing her the bag. "Casson texted that you had come over with some cookies. I couldn't get here fast enough," he laughed.

"Hey, what's so funny out there?" Casson's

voice boomed from the kitchen. "Come on in; coffee's on."

Ronnie stepped back to let Red in. She set the bag down by the door. He hung up his parka and followed her to the kitchen, where Casson was filling a mug. He set it on the island and then walked over to shake Red's hand.

"Have a seat there, Mr. Brannigan," he said, grinning, "and grab a cookie."

"Only one?" Red complained. He tilted his head toward Ronnie on the stool next to his. "Perhaps I can find a way to convince your cousin here to perform an act of charity and make me a batch of my own…"

"Good luck with that," Casson laughed. At Amy Jay's sudden wail, he excused himself to assume his parental responsibilities.

"I should head back to the cottage, Cass," Ronnie said. "I still have boxes all over the place."

"What? You're leaving, too? Is it something I said?" Red held his half-eaten cookie in midair. "If you both desert me, I'll have to drown my sorrows by eating the rest of these cookies."

"I'll let *you* handle this drama," Casson laughed, giving Ronnie a hug. "See you later."

Red's gaze swept over Ronnie. She had

changed into a pair of maroon jeans and a black long-sleeved shirt that accentuated her feminine curves. An inner voice prompted him to offer to help her with the unpacking. He started to open his mouth, and then he snapped it shut.

Stay away, Brannigan, his common sense warned. *You'd be entering a danger zone. Remember your vow? She has a child. You can't take this kind of a risk. Don't. Get. Involved.*

Ronnie was looking at him quizzically. "I *did* end up with some extra cookies," she said nonchalantly. "You can have them, if you'd like."

Something leaped in his chest. He blinked wordlessly for a moment, then nodded. "I'll just take care of some business with Casson, and then I'll come by."

Common sense be damned, he thought, watching her leave. What fool would pass up a batch of her cookies?

CHAPTER NINE

RONNIE'S HEART WAS pounding all the way back to her cottage, and it wasn't due to exertion from speed-walking or running. She had barely acknowledged the fact that it had started to snow, and when she arrived, she was surprised at the snowflakes that had accumulated on her coat and hood. She quickly removed her coat and boots, and after setting her bag of books down on the kitchen table, she hurried to put the cooled cookies in a small tin. She would hand them to Red as soon as he arrived, then he would be on his way, she would close the door, and she would have the rest of the evening to herself.

She peered out the window of the front door. No sign of him yet. She caught a glimpse of herself in the small oval mirror on the wall adjacent to the door. Her hair was wind-tossed, her cheeks were rosy and her eyes looked darker than usual. She patted down her hair and walked over to turn on the gas fireplace. She sat down on the edge of the couch and picked up the *Parry Sound Life* magazine on the coffee table, flipping through the pages but not really processing what she was seeing.

The sound of wheels crunching along her driveway startled Ronnie. She stood up and then promptly sat down. She picked up the magazine again, and a few moments later she heard the knock. Taking a deep breath, she walked to the door and saw Red's profile through the transparent curtain. She opened the door. Red had his hood off and the plump snowflakes were drifting onto his head and face.

"Hi again, Ronnie," he said, smiling.

"Hi." She noticed that he hadn't left his truck running...

"May I come in?" He shook the snow off his hair and shoulders.

"Um, sure," she said, stepping back awkwardly. She hadn't intended for him to come in, but how could she say no?

Red closed the door behind him and stood on the mat. Ronnie saw him scanning the boxes piled along the living room wall, and then his gaze shifted to the kitchen counter where she had placed the tin.

"I'll grab the cookies," she said. As she began to move toward the kitchen area, he put a hand on her arm.

"Hold on, Ronnie. I *did* come here for your cookies, but I also wanted to ask you something."

"Oh?" Ronnie frowned.

"Would you like some help?"

"Help? With what?"

He pointed to the boxes. "With *those*. Unpacking can be a drag when you have to do it by yourself. Besides," he added with a glint in his eye, "I need to perform my one good deed of the day."

"Says who?" She looked at him skeptically.

"It's a universal law," he said. "Has to be done—" he checked his watch "—by 5:00 p.m. Which means I still have time."

"I'm sure you have more important things to do with your time, Mr. Brannigan. But if you're willing to help, I'd be silly to say no. So...yes, I'll accept your offer. You can hang your coat up on that hook."

While Red took off his parka and boots, Ronnie went over and transferred a few boxes from the stack near the wall to the living room carpet. She opened the first box, labeled BOOKS. "Those can go on the mantel for now," she told him. There was actually a bookshelf in her bedroom, but she felt awkward sending him there.

She grabbed the second box labeled in red crayon with Andy's name and smiled. He had wanted to help pack his things, and she had indulged him. He hadn't quite followed any particular folding technique, but that hadn't bothered her. She had watched him out of the corner of her eye, proud of her little guy as he rolled up pants and shirts, socks and underwear. And she had been both amused and touched when he had raced to get one of his plush animals to pack into each box, hugging them before closing the box.

Red had finished unpacking the books and had knelt on one knee across from her. She handed him Andy's box.

"You can unpack this directly into the chest of drawers in Andy's room," she said. "Down the hall, first door on your right."

Ronnie saw something flicker in Red's eyes. Was that a look of dismay? His smile faded for a mere second before he smiled brightly, making her dismiss her initial notion. It must have been the play of light on his face…

Red took the box and strode down the hall, his jaw muscles tensing. He had gotten himself into this, and now he had no choice but to carry it through.

He stole a sideways look at Ronnie before entering Andy's room. She had opened another book box and was looking through the pile she had lifted out, her lips curved into a smile. Red stepped into the boy's room. The comforter on the twin bed had a space theme, showing planets and galaxies and shooting stars. A plush bear was plopped against the bed pillow, and instead of the usual pads on its paws, four red hearts had been sewn on. Another heart filled the center of the bear's chest. Red felt a twinge in his chest. Had Ronnie bought Andy the bear while he was at SickKids? He set down the box and he picked up the bear. It was soft, and Red found himself pressing it against his cheek.

That was when he felt his own heart crack. He had given Marco a bear for his fourth birthday, only it was much bigger, like an actual bear cub, and Marco had wanted it placed in a corner of his room, near his bookshelf. When Red had asked him to think of a name, Marco had scrunched up his face and tapped his chin, and suddenly, he had grinned from ear to ear. "Red!"

"Yes?" Red had replied and Marco had laughed. "No, I'm calling my bear 'Red'!

That way, you'll always be with me, even when you're not!" And then he had plopped himself down into the bear's lap and asked Red to read him a story before bedtime.

Red had laughed at the time, but now the memory sent sharp spears into his chest.

How could he not foresee that Andy's toys would trigger such memories?

He had to get himself out of there...

When Red had impulsively jumped at Ronnie's offer, he had been thinking primarily about himself. And not just because he'd be ending up with a batch of her cookies. If he had to be completely honest with himself, the main reason was that he'd get to see Ronnie alone again. In *her* space.

Something was drawing him to her, and he was having a hard time resisting the magnetic pull. Now, immersed in memories activated by entering Andy's room, Red felt regret washing over him. He looked down at the box that he had set down.

Just do it, his inner voice prompted.

He strode to the dresser and pulled open the top drawer. He tried to swallow the lump in his throat from handling each rolled-up little item. This was exactly why he should have heeded his common sense and stayed away.

He couldn't handle this. At least not now.

Too many emotions were surfacing, feelings that he had convinced himself were resolved when it came to Marco…

He had to leave.

He would tell Ronnie that he had a very important meeting in Toronto with a client from Melbourne the day after tomorrow, and he needed to go over the files.

It *was* true. There was no way he could tell her the real reason…

Red returned to the living room with the empty box. He saw Ronnie perched on a chair by the fireplace, arranging some books on the mantel. His gaze fell on one chair leg, positioned unevenly on the raised edge around the porcelain tiles at the base of the fireplace. When he saw it start to wobble a moment later, he let the box drop and leaped to prevent Ronnie from falling. The chair tipped and fell over, but Ronnie was already in his arms.

She had let out a cry at his sudden intervention, and her arms had instinctively entwined themselves around his neck. For a timeless moment, their gazes locked and their bodies pressed against each other. He couldn't tell if the wildly beating heart was his or hers. Her eyes were dark pools, their pupils expanded. He wished he could read their impenetrable depths…

And then he had no choice but to release his hold around her waist, letting her slide down his body until her feet touched the floor.

"Sorry," he said gruffly, righting the chair. "You could have fallen and hit your head on those tiles." He pointed to the raised border around the tiles. "The chair leg wasn't positioned on the flat part."

"Thanks," she said breathlessly. "I feel like such a klutz. I seem to lose my balance every time I'm around you," she added accusingly.

"And fortunately for you, I've been successful in preventing you from falling," he replied smoothly. "You might want to consider protecting yourself with bubble wrap as a preventative measure," he said with a crooked smile, gesturing toward a pile of it in a box Ronnie had unpacked previously. "Especially since I can't stick around to save you again."

Her brow furrowed momentarily, and she took a step back. "No problem. I wouldn't want to keep inconveniencing you," she replied tersely. "I'm sure I can manage to save myself."

"No inconven—"

"I'll get your cookies." She turned away sharply and returned with the tin, avoiding his gaze.

She had taken offence at his words. But what had he said that could have bothered her?

"Thanks, Ronnie. I have a very important meeting coming up in Toronto and—"

"You don't need to explain. It's none of my business." She crossed in front of him to open the door, letting in a snowy gust of wind.

She was figuratively and literally giving him the cold shoulder. He brushed the snow off him and bent to put on his boots before reaching for his parka on the wall hook.

She obviously didn't want him around...

"Thanks for your help," she said stiffly, holding out the cookies.

"No problem," he said, attempting to sound casual. "Good night, and thank *you*." As he stepped up into his truck, he glanced back at the cottage. He waited a few moments, then turned on the ignition and drove away. What had he expected? That Ronnie would rush to the window and wave him off?

Don't be a fool, he scoffed inwardly. And why would he expect or want Ronnie to do such a thing?

On the way home, his thoughts vaulted between his reaction in Andy's room to what it felt like holding Ronnie in his arms. He tried to divert his thoughts to what he hoped would be accomplished at his upcoming meeting in Toronto with the Australian tycoon. If all went as planned, he'd be approving a billion-dollar account, toasting the success of the project, and then driving back to Parry Sound for the rest of his holiday.

With one important event on the agenda at the end of the month: the grand opening of Franklin's Resort.

The thought of the resort made his thoughts return to Andy, and how being in his room had triggered emotions he thought he had resolved. Red wondered what Marco was doing now. Had his mother flown to Italy with him over the summer? Had she decided which school to enroll him in? Was Marco happy? Did the boy ever ask about him? Did he think about Red whenever he looked at his bear?

Red clenched his jaw. He had to stop. Stop wondering. Stop tormenting himself. Marco was young. He wouldn't have suffered from the loss in the same way Red had suffered... Or had he?

Maybe he needed to talk to somebody about this. He had believed that he had worked through his grief, but putting himself right into another child's space and doing the seemingly innocuous task of putting away some of

Andy's clothes and picking up his plush toy had rocketed some feelings that he had obviously buried right back to the surface…

What he *didn't* need to do was get himself tied up in a relationship when a child was in the picture. And although there was no relationship between him and Ronnie, why tempt fate and let himself get drawn into her life? She had moved to Parry Sound permanently, and *his* permanent home base was Toronto. He'd be back more often now that he had bought the Victorian mansion and was making plans to renovate it, but with his business dealings and travel around the world, he couldn't see himself even considering a long-distance relationship with anyone.

But even more than these kinds of logistics, Red had to seriously consider whether he could risk encouraging a relationship with Ronnie and consequently getting close to her little boy…a boy who could end up with a relapse. Could he face that kind of responsibility? The uncertainty? Could he allow himself to open his heart to the kid—as he had done with Marco—and then risk having it broken again if Andy—

No! He wasn't even going to go there…

At home, Red got a fire going, poured himself a brandy and sat by the fire and stared into the flames. He could repress some of his fears, but he honestly had to search his soul to see if he could cope with such a dire situation... Or would he end up quitting on her, like her ex-husband had done?

No again! He was not that kind of a guy...

But one part of him was pulling him one way, and the other was pulling him in the other direction. Red swallowed the last of his brandy. He was in a tug of war. With himself.

He'd eventually have to let go...

Letting out a soft growl, he strode to his desk and opened his laptop. He needed the distraction of work to blot out the duel playing out in his brain.

CHAPTER TEN

RONNIE CONTROLLED THE impulse to go to the window. She heard Red's truck starting up and driving off, and when she was sure he was out of sight, she went and looked out. It was still snowing and the image of Red at her door earlier, shaking the snowflakes off his head and shoulders, made her heart skip a beat. Again. His physical presence moments later in the cottage had made the space suddenly seem smaller.

She had been very conscious of his proximity as she opened up the boxes and handed him the books. A couple of times, her fingers had brushed against his, and she had deliberately avoided glancing at him. But she hadn't been able to avoid meeting his gaze when her chair had caught the edge around the tiled fireplace base and he had leaped to prevent her from falling.

It had happened so quickly. Her brain had

hardly registered that the chair was tilting when his arms reached out and braced themselves around her waist. The few seconds that it had taken for him to do that and then set her down had, at the time, seemed to play out in slow motion...

Her initial gasp as his strong arms closed around her had given way to a heavy heart thumping at the impact of her body being pressed against his. Her eyes had melted into the mesmerizing landscape of his eyes. And the slow, *very slow*, descent of her body sliding down his had sent a surge pulsating throughout all her nerve endings.

And was sending a shiver through her now...

Her reaction to his proximity was one-sided, no doubt.

Ronnie searched her memory to find out if Casson had mentioned Red having a current girlfriend or having been married. Of course he hadn't. Casson hadn't shared much about Red, other than the fact that he was a friend from university, and that it was *his* firm that would be designing Franklin's Resort.

She pictured the woman who would most likely be Red's type: tall like him, probably, wearing exclusive fashions and mingling in upscale social circles. She could see the woman linking her arm with his as they strode into an invitation-only event at Roy Thomson Hall or some private party after a movie premiere at the Toronto International Film Festival, rocking her European designer gown and killer heels.

Would. You. Stop!

Why on earth was she even spending any energy on such thoughts? What difference did it make to her whom he was seeing?

Ronnie sauntered to the kitchen and scanned the contents of the fridge. She wasn't really in the mood to cook anything. She fixed herself a peanut butter and jam sandwich and ate it at the kitchen table while looking through some files on her laptop related to her new position as Provincial Marketing Manager for the Forrest Hardware chain. She was looking forward to working from home, with occasional trips to the stores across the province. Some of her out-of-town meetings could be accomplished in a day trip while others might take a couple of days or more. She was happy that with both scenarios, she could leave Andy in Casson's and Justine's capable hands.

Ronnie looked forward to using her university training and skills in this new position. She smiled. She was excited about starting her new job and implementing some of the innovative marketing strategies she had been working on.

Ronnie finished the last bite of her sandwich and her glass of milk. She shut down her laptop and reached for the bag of books, and immediately the image of Red popped into her mind.

Well, she didn't want Red in her mind. He had already taken up too much of her headspace…

Ronnie sauntered over to the living room and set the books on the coffee table before going to her bedroom to change into her pajamas. She would relax with one of her new books for a bit until she felt ready to go to bed.

Moments later she curled up on one corner of the couch. Pulling the books out of the bag, she smiled at the cover of the one she had picked up for Andy. She would enjoy reading it together with him soon. Ronnie set aside the Giller Prize–winning book, wanting to savor it when she had a bigger block of time. She stared at the title of the next book. *Moving On: Embracing a New Chapter of Your Life*. Hmm. Did she really want to get into that now? She reread the blurb on the back cover and skimmed over the table of contents.

Serious stuff.

She could actually skip over the first three chapters. She had accepted the past and looked at her options, which had led to the packing up and moving out theme of chapter three. Now she considered herself happily at the unpacking stage.

Ronnie yawned. She'd pick one chapter to read and then call it a night. But which one? Her gaze flew over the next few chapter headings and stopped at chapter seven, *Learning to Trust Again*. Was she ready to do that? Did she want to?

Trusting again… That implied a desire or readiness to invest in a new relationship. Which meant that reading this chapter would just bring Red back into her headspace… whether she liked it or not.

Red had said he didn't have a "significant other" and had referred to himself as "once burned, twice shy." And then he had gone on to say that he had been "scorched." She couldn't see him being ready to trust again. Why would he want to get involved with someone else after such a terrible experience?

Why would she? After all, like Ronnie had said to Red, they weren't exactly knocking at her door.

Well, not "they," actually. Just Red.

And all he had wanted was her peanut butter cookies. Not her.

With a wistful sigh, she started to read the chapter anyway…

Red shut down his laptop and got ready for bed. Minutes later he was staring at the ceiling, his brain a jumble of conflicting thoughts. Maybe he should have had a cup of herbal tea instead of the brandy…

Impatiently, he threw back the covers. Running his fingers through his hair, he strode to the large casement window that overlooked the expanse of pond. Snowflakes were drifting gently down, occasionally sticking to the window. They were tiny and intricate. Beautiful.

Like Ronnie…

But out of reach.

The metaphorical glass between them was a little boy. No—two little boys. Andy and Marco.

Andy was Ronnie's shield against the intrusion of another man in her life—or so he had inferred from her comments about Andy being her priority. And even though Marco was no longer in his life physically, he was still in Red's mind…and heart…

A knot nudged its way into his throat, helped along by twinges of guilt.

Perhaps he should have never encouraged Marco to get so close to him. Maybe he should have kept his distance more, until he and Sofia had been on the same page when it came to their feelings for each other.

He had assumed too much. He had thought that once she had taken care of business in Italy, they would move forward in their relationship.

Red felt a surge of anger shoot through him. He had been so naive when it came to Sofia. He had trusted her, believed her when she had told him that all those trips back to Italy were absolutely necessary. Four trips in two months…

He gave a cynical laugh. What a fool he had been!

And he had innocently encouraged the bond between himself and Marco to grow…

How could he not feel guilt now over the fact that it must have exacerbated the loss and confusion Marco would have felt at Red's sudden disappearance from his life?

Red turned away from the window. Sofia hadn't been the only one to blame in all this. He had to accept his share of it, even though he had only ever had the best of intentions when it had come to Marco...

Taking a deep breath, he walked to his dresser and picked up the photo of him and Marco. He stared at it for a long time, forcing himself to accept his conflicting feelings. He really had no choice but to move forward with his life...

The photo became blurry. "I'm so sorry, Marco," he rasped. "I never wanted to hurt you." He set it back down, wiped his eyes and went to bed.

CHAPTER ELEVEN

FROM THE BRIGHTNESS in her room, Ronnie realized that she had slept in. She had obviously needed it. She stretched languorously before reaching for her cell phone on her night table to check the time. Nine twenty…

She padded to the living room and looked out the bay window. Last night's snow and wind had come to a stop. The surface of the bay and the dense woodlands beyond the blanketed shoreline were glistening with pinpoints of sunlight. It would be a perfect day to go for a walk in the woods—do some "forest bathing," as she had heard it called. Refresh her mind and spirit out in nature. Maybe she'd even spot a snowshoe hare or a fox…

You have work to do, her inner slave driver reminded her. *Boxes to unpack, shelves to line, clothes to hang, laundry to do…*

She would put on some coffee, have some toast and head out. The work wasn't going anywhere, but she was! Passing by the coffee table on her way to the kitchen, Ronnie's gaze dropped to the book she had been reading last night and the chapter about learning to trust again.

She stooped to pick up the book, then changed her mind and continued on to the kitchen. She didn't want to think about trusting, or taking chances, or anything that had to do with contemplating a new relationship. There was no contender presently in her life, nor was there the possibility of anything changing soon. After the weeklong stay at Franklin's Resort, she would be starting a job that would require some traveling back and forth to Toronto, and when she wasn't doing that, she'd be at home in Parry Sound. Hopefully, once she was in a routine, and after the snow melted, she could start looking for a place of her own.

Casson and Justine had actually offered to sell her the cottage she was staying in...and she *was* seriously considering it. It would be great to be close to family. By spring, Justine's mom and dad would be back from their three-month vacation in Arizona, and Justine had already told Ronnie that her parents would also be happy to babysit Andy when Ronnie was out of town.

And Winter's Haven was a fabulous property. Cottages were in high demand in Parry Sound and Georgian Bay. Cottagers who lived in Toronto and tourists caused the town's population to soar in the summer. Casson had mentioned that the few property owners who *were* willing to sell their cottages, were getting their asking price or even higher. Buyers were willing to pay the big bucks for cottages on the pristine waters of either Georgian Bay or the many inland lakes. They could enjoy the natural beauty of mixed woodlands, smooth or granite shorelines and breathtaking sunsets under a canopy of stars on a sultry summer night.

She had it made, she thought, putting on the coffee. Her little boy was in good health, her family was close by and so supportive, and she was about to start a big new job. What more could she want?

A man, maybe? A little voice edged its way into her thoughts. *Companionship? Love?*

The two slices of bread she had plunked in the toaster popped up, startling her. She brushed away her thoughts and focused on buttering her toast and filling her mug with coffee.

As she ate her breakfast, Ronnie's gaze took in the cozy ambiance of the cottage. Maybe she *would* stay put here for a while. Enjoy the seasons as they changed. Go cross-country skiing, ice fishing, swimming, blueberry picking, hiking… And in a few minutes, a glorious walk through the forested property.

Ronnie put her dish and mug in the sink and went to change out of her pajamas. She *was* moving forward, like the blurb said on the back cover of her book, and embracing the new chapter in her life.

The only thing she didn't have in her life was *someone* to embrace…

Red thanked Casson and Justine and put on the snowmobile helmet. Casson had said he could try his snowmobile out, and he had, several times since he had arrived in Parry Sound. Red had enjoyed riding along the Seguin Trail, which, Casson had told him, linked sledders all across Ontario. Red was happy to have been introduced to a new adventure into a winter wonderland of snow-frosted forests and ice-etched lakes and rivers, a magical place when the sun glinted through the evergreen canopies onto the smooth trail route. Red planned to purchase a sled of his own to enjoy on winter weekends in Parry Sound in the future.

He had woken up this morning with the intention of getting some fresh air on the trail. Once he had arrived at Winter's Haven, he had had a coffee with Casson and Justine, and as he was getting ready to head out on the sled, Justine had innocently suggested that he ask Ronnie to go sledding with him.

He had looked blankly at Justine for a moment and then at Casson, who had shrugged and given him a silent *I don't know what that's all about* look.

"Um… I don't know if she'd even be interested in—"

"She needs a little fun in her life," Justine urged. "It's a double seater, and she can borrow my helmet." And she had swiftly pulled it out of the hall closet before handing it to Red.

After thanking them, he climbed aboard the red-and-black snowmobile and headed to Ronnie's cottage. How had he allowed himself to be roped into this situation? Could he not have just said "No"?

He stopped the machine and in a few strides he was at her door. He gave a couple of knocks, and then another couple of knocks, and when she didn't answer, he figured she was either sleeping or pretending she didn't hear the door. And then he noticed her boot prints on the steps leading in the opposite direction from the way he had come.

Red considered his options. Return the helmet to Justine or head out in the direction of the tracks Ronnie had left.

Another mental tug of war...

He sighed, put his helmet back on and moments later was following Ronnie's trail.

A mile down the road, he spotted her. She was staring up at something in a tree, and as he approached, she turned to watch him. Red brought the machine to a stop and pulled off his helmet.

"Oh! I thought you were Casson!" She frowned.

"Understandable mistake," he drawled. "Are you enjoying your walk?"

"I am," she said. "Actually, I was enjoying the solitude and quiet of the forest..."

"Forgive me for the raucous intrusion."

At that moment a blue jay let out a squawk. "Hey, it's getting really noisy out here. Want to go for a ride?" Red gave her a tentative grin.

Ronnie looked at him as if he had suggested something improper. "Have you had enough practice on that beast?" she said doubtfully.

"Well, if you don't trust me, why don't you take the reins?"

Her brows furrowed. "Um...don't be offended, but...okay, I will!" She took the helmet and Red caught the sudden gleam in her eyes.

"Should I be afraid?" he laughed, handing her Justine's helmet.

Her brows arched but she didn't respond. "Give it up, Brannigan," she told him, with a curl of her lip.

Red scooted back in his seat.

Ronnie checked the throttle and turned the key to start the engine. When it was idling smoothly, Red had just enough time to straighten in his seat before she zoomed off, sending a spray of snow over him from both sides.

CHAPTER TWELVE

Ronnie had no idea what had come over her...deciding to take Red up on his offer of a ride, and then impulsively taking the driver's seat. Something had risen up inside her, made her want to show Red that she was in control of her life, that she was perfectly capable of taking charge...

She had had plenty of practice riding on and driving a snowmobile in the past throughout the Muskoka trails, especially before Andy was born, and the temptation to show Red her ability—given that he was a relative newbie at sledding—had been too hard to resist.

What she hadn't initially thought through was the fact that the Viking would be pressed against her, his hands alternating from the side hand rests to her waist...

She had tried to ignore the sensation of having Red so close, and focus instead on the exhilaration of the ride with the sun streaming over them and the dazzling views of the woodlands on either side of them as they sped by. Ronnie had done the loop through Winter's Haven and then proceeded to the route that led to the Seguin Trail. After about a forty-five-minute run, they were back in front of Ronnie's cottage.

Red climbed off the sled, pulled off his helmet and waited for Ronnie to do the same. He nodded slowly with an enigmatic smile, and she smiled back, the adrenaline still pumping through her.

"Thanks for the thrills and chills," he said dryly. "I'd invite myself over for some hot chocolate, but I have some business files to look through. So I'd better take the sled back and head home..." His eyes narrowed. "But you'll have to show me a little trust the next time, Ronnie, and let *me* drive..."

Her pulse skipping a beat at his words, Ronnie watched him drive away. Once inside, she immersed herself under a hot shower and unsuccessfully tried to put Red out of her mind. But how could she when she had felt his Viking presence both physically and emotionally on the snowmobile...

Ronnie's cell phone rang, startling her. She saw that it was Casson and reached over to put the phone on speaker mode. "Hey, Cass, what's up?"

"Hi, Ronnie. I need you to do me a favor…"

"Sure; do you need me to babysit A.J.?"

"No, it's not that. The baby's running a fever, and Justine thinks *she's* coming down with something, too."

"Oh, my goodness, what can I do to help?"

"How do you feel about starting your new position sooner? Like tomorrow. I have a meeting with the Toronto store manager to discuss some of those new marketing plans outlined in the file I sent you two days ago. But I don't want to leave Justine and the baby. It's just for tomorrow, Ronnie. You can take over completely when you actually start in a month's time."

Ronnie thought fast. She'd have to get up at the crack of dawn to either beat or join the early-morning commuters going to Toronto. She had really hoped to sleep in and have a leisurely day unpacking the remaining boxes and then going for a long country walk. But she'd have to delay those plans now. There was no way she could turn Cass down. She didn't blame him for wanting to stay close to his wife and baby in their time of need. That's what a devoted husband and father did…

"Of course I'll go, dear cousin. You just

worry about taking care of your beautiful girls. I've got this."

"I know you do, Ronnie. By the way, when I was talking with Red earlier he mentioned that he was heading to Toronto tomorrow morning for a meeting himself. I hope you don't mind, Ronnie, but I just gave him a quick call a minute ago—hopeful that you would say yes— and asked if he wouldn't mind driving you also, since you're both heading downtown. It'll be safer traveling in his truck."

Ronnie's brain swirled with this sudden rush of information. "What did he say?" she said, keeping her voice casual.

"He said it would be his pleasure…and that *he* would drive," Casson chuckled.

"Um…*okay* then." Her cheeks burned at the knowledge that Red had told Casson about their ride…

"Thanks, Ronnie. I'll keep you posted about the girls."

"Give them hugs for me, okay?"

"Will do, and, oh, Red said to be ready by 6:00 a.m. sharp. He'll be waiting outside 'with bells on.'"

Ronnie set her cell phone down. The thought of traveling with Red for a couple of hours to Toronto and back in such proximity sent a series of bells clanging in her chest…

* * *

Red's personal black limo pulled up to the estate at the exact time he had specified to the driver the night before after deciding against taking his own truck. "Good morning, Liam," Red said, as the driver stepped out of the limo.

"Top of the morning to you, sir!"

As Liam briskly opened the door for him, Red placed his garment bag and black leather briefcase in the back seat. He would change before his meeting in his Toronto office. Pulling up the collar of his jacket, Red got in and put on his seat belt before giving Liam directions to Ronnie's cottage. It was dark, as dark as it had been at midnight when he had still been up, thinking about Casson's request the evening before.

Since returning home yesterday, all Red could think about was the rush he had felt riding on the sled with Ronnie, and how his intentions to keep his distance from her always seemed to go awry. He had just finished choosing his suit and tie for the next day when his phone had buzzed.

Casson had explained what he needed and Red had groaned inwardly. It seemed that every time he had convinced himself to stay away from Ronnie, the universe contrived to throw them together.

Red hadn't been able to come up with a reason why he couldn't take Ronnie with him. "No problem," he had told Casson, making an effort to keep his voice light.

Of course it was a problem.

But he couldn't turn Casson down, even if it meant being thrown together with Ronnie for a good part of a day. Casson had thanked him and promised to have him over for his homemade chili one night soon.

Red had hung up the garment bag with his suit in the foyer armoire, leaving the door open so he wouldn't forget it in the morning. Shortly after, he had tried to push away thoughts about Ronnie while he was going over his files, but their constant intrusion had forced him to shut down his laptop.

He had poured himself a brandy and had tried to process the impact of Ronnie Forrester in his life since he had stopped to rescue her. He had only known her for a little over forty-eight hours, but Ronnie had landed in Parry Sound like a meteorite, making a sizable dent on the surface and sending chunks flying in every direction.

And one of those chunks had hit *him*. *Hard*.

Red had swallowed the rest of his brandy

and headed to his en suite bathroom for a quick shower, the quickest he could manage, so he wouldn't be tormented by the memory of his body pressed against hers...

He hadn't been successful. The torment had been sweet, and the possibility of his imaginings becoming a reality had steamed up his consciousness more than the way the hot water had steamed up the shower.

Afterward, he had put on a robe and decided against driving to Toronto himself. He would employ the services of his private limo driver...

Liam now turned into the winding road that led to Ronnie's cottage. His pulse spiked when Liam made the last turn. Ronnie was waiting at her doorstep, wearing a short red coat over a dark gray dress or skirt, and short black dress boots. She had a red-and-black scarf tied around her neck, and her black winter cap matched her black gloves. She had a briefcase that she had set down, and was peering down the driveway, her eyes widening as the limo glided toward her.

Well, at least she was on time. "I'll get her door," he told Liam.

"Good morning, Ronnie." He opened the door on the passenger side for her and held out his hand to take her briefcase, which he set down on the seat opposite his. Red tried not to let his gaze linger over the way her dress or skirt tapered to just inches above her knees, and at the generous glimpse of her legs below... He held out his hand, instinctively guessing that she might need it to prevent slipping, especially with those heels...

"Good morning." Ronnie took his gloved hand and gave him an awkward smile as she stepped into the limo, her cheeks flushed.

CHAPTER THIRTEEN

"I HOPE CASSON warned you about my strict rules for passengers who travel with me," Red said wryly, while he buckled up across from her.

Ronnie's eyebrows shot up. "Actually, just one. And I *did* comply, being outside at the precise time you had specified. Although I had expected you to drive up in your truck, not in *this*."

"I appreciated that," he said, nodding to Liam through the glass partition to proceed. "Although, if I was driving by myself, I would have probably left at least an hour earlier."

Ronnie stared at his profile, wondering if he was annoyed with having had to alter his plans to include her. She caught the slight tensing of his jaw muscles. He *was* annoyed.

"Well, Casson didn't have to go and ask you to include me in your travel plans," she blurted defensively. "I would have been okay to travel on my own… You'd think he was my parent at times, instead of my cousin, worrying so much about me."

Red glanced at her, his brow furrowing. "Well, you *did* have a recent incident with your vehicle," he reminded her pointedly. "But no need to bring up the past. You might as well sit back and enjoy the ride."

Ronnie stifled the response she wanted to articulate and settled back against the plush leather upholstery, wishing she had thought to sit next to Red, instead of having to face him the whole trip. It was disconcerting. His face scruff had undergone some trimming. If he had been good-looking before, now he could join the ranks of hunks in magazines, or in commercials for high-end cologne… And whatever cologne he was wearing at the moment, the refreshing scent of pine trees, seemed to be encapsulated in the limo with them.

"Can I get the driver to stop at a coffee shop before we hit the highway?" He slid open a temperature-controlled compartment in the limo that held bottles of champagne, wine and assorted liquors. An adjacent section held a variety of fluted and other glasses.

"I don't imagine you'd be up for one of these."
A corner of his mouth curved upward.

"You imagine correctly," she said curtly.
"That's not my style."

Red switched on the intercom and instructed Liam to stop at the coffee shop coming up on their right.

"Large coffee your style?" He glanced at Ronnie.

"Yes, thanks. Double milk, no sugar," she said, zipping open her handbag to grab her change purse.

"I think I can handle paying for an extra cup of coffee," he said, grinning.

"I didn't want to be presumptuous," she said, lifting her chin. "But I *will* split the limo bill with you."

"No worries," he laughed, "I've saved for that, as well. Are you hungry? Can I get you anything else?"

Ronnie shook her head. "No, thanks. I'll wait until we get to Toronto."

As the driving resumed out of town and onto the highway heading south, Ronnie sipped her coffee and kept her gaze outside the window. The traffic wasn't bad; they would feel it in about an hour, though, once they approached Barrie. From there on, it would be pretty congested alongside the regular commuters.

Ronnie stole a glance at Red. He seemed immersed in thought, and she wondered if it had something to do with his business in Toronto. Her gaze dropped to his wool jacket, blue checkered shirt and jeans. She had noticed the garment bag hanging up next to him and imagined what he'd look like in a suit and tie. Something dark would be perfect for him, she thought. Pine or teal green. Or classic black. With that hair of his, he'd look—

"Are you all set for your meeting?"

Her head snapped up to meet his. A transport truck drove by them, illuminating them both for a few moments. Ronnie was mortified, having been caught staring. She could feel a spiral of heat rising to her neck and cheeks.

"I'm as ready as I can be," she said lightly. "My job as Provincial Marketing Manager will officially start in about a month. I'll go at it full tilt then."

"I'm sure you will. Congratulations. Casson had told me about your new position."

"Thanks. Um…what time is *your* meeting? Maybe I'll have time to do a little shopping. My son's birthday is coming up." She bit her lip, a wave of emotion engulfing her. This birthday would be different. Finally. Gratitude for the end of Andy's maintenance treatment. And joy in the miracle of his remission. Ronnie turned to look out her window, her eyes misting. The sudden raucous honking of horns jarred her back to the moment, and she turned in alarm.

"Just a couple of idiots trying to pass a transport truck," Red said, shaking his head. He gave her a look of reassurance. "Don't worry; you're in good hands." He looked away before she could.

She was glad, because her cheeks were flaming as an image of herself in *his* hands, or rather, in his arms, as she had been two—no, *three*—times now, popped into her mind. Despite the coffee, she felt fatigue from too little sleep last night weighing down her eyelids. She had woken up twice during the night, and when the alarm had finally gone off, she had bolted out of bed, afraid to press on the snooze button in case she slept through the next alarm. She had had a quick shower, dried and brushed her hair, and gotten dressed in less than half an hour. And she had been out the door with her briefcase in hand two minutes before Red had appeared.

She had stood in the frosty stillness, looking up at the black sky and breathing in the crisp pine-scented air. Inhaling and exhaling deeply, she had felt a sense of peace come over her. And a tingle of anticipation at the same time. She looked forward to the upcoming meeting, and afterward, exploring some of the shops in the area to find something special for Andy's birthday.

While she was picturing Andy's little face shining with pleasure as he was about to blow out his birthday candles, the sleek limousine had appeared in the driveway. For a few moments, his headlights had blinded her and she had stood there stunned, having expected Red to drive up in his truck. She still hadn't moved when Red had jumped out to open the door on her side of the vehicle.

As she had handed Red her briefcase, Ronnie hadn't missed his gaze casually sweeping over her.

And approval in the dark, enigmatic depths of his eyes…

Red gazed at the woman across from him. She had removed her coat and had fallen asleep just before Barrie, an hour from Toronto. Her arms were crisscrossed against her chest. She looked so vulnerable, her long lashes resting on her face like a…like a sleeping angel.

His gaze dropped to the locket around her

neck. He hadn't noticed it earlier. The latch wasn't completely closed and the locket had opened to reveal a tiny photo. Her son. On the other side, nothing.

Had it previously held the photo of her husband?

He felt his jaw muscles tightening. Why did he feel so conflicted?

You know why, his inner voice murmured. *You're attracted to Ronnie, but you don't want to be. Because of her little boy...*

Red glanced again at the photo. A feeling of guilt washed over him. The kid didn't deserve this kind of rejection. Neither did Ronnie. They both deserved to have someone who could accept them both. *Together.*

It was just too bad that *he* had had such a heartbreaking experience in the past. An experience that was affecting his choices now. The choice to risk again.

There was only one thing stopping him. *Fear.*

The realization stunned him.

Fear had essentially kept him from even considering another relationship since his breakup with Sofia. He had purposefully buried himself in work so as not to even be tempted to get involved with another woman. Why would he? He had been burned.

Scorched. And he hadn't been ready to trust again.

Fear had succeeded in freezing his emotions. But something was changing. Something was chipping away at the hard layer of ice that had formed around his heart. Or rather, someone.

Ronnie Forrester. Even though she wasn't aware that she was holding a hammer and chisel…

He saw Ronnie shifting in her seat and the movement roused her. She glanced out the window. The sky had lightened and she blinked before checking her watch. "Wow. I—I guess I needed that snooze."

"No worries. That's part of the passenger perks," he said, flashing her a teasing grin.

She responded with a crooked smile and noticing her open locket, she clasped it and snapped it shut.

Red saw her briefly hold up the locket to her cheek. She was such a devoted mother. That little boy was everything to her. And Red knew she was the kind of mother who would put Andy's needs and welfare before her own.

He felt an overwhelming desire to gather her up in his arms and just hold her. Cradle her against his chest and show her how much he respected her for everything she had done for her son. For her selfless, loving presence and care. She was the kind of mother every child should have. The kind of mother he wished he had had when he was young.

The kind of mother he'd want for his children...

CHAPTER FOURTEEN

THE LIMO STOPPED and dropped Ronnie off right at the Yonge Street store. Since Red's meeting was scheduled at the same time, he had suggested they join up afterward for lunch. When he had found out she had never been to 360, the CN Tower revolving restaurant, he called and made reservations. "Might as well do something new while you're in town," he said. "Good luck with your meeting."

An hour later, Ronnie walked out of the hardware store with a light heart. Mr. Kennedy had been very open and receptive to what she had to show him. He thanked her for being Casson's emissary and told her that he would arrange a final conference with Casson.

Ronnie headed toward the downtown area. She had time to peruse a few shops before heading to the CN Tower. She ambled along

Yonge Street near Bay. Ronnie wasn't sure what she was looking for, but she was determined to go back to the cottage with something unique that Andy could cherish forever.

Ronnie arrived at the Eaton Centre. She would surely find something here, she thought, striding toward the navigation screen that listed the stores and boutiques on each level. She searched for children's novelty shops, made a note of where they were located and set off.

Ronnie entered a children's store that, at first glance, seemed to offer a wide variety of gifts. She walked up and down the aisles slowly, hoping something extraordinary would catch her eye.

And it did, near the back of the store. Her eyes widened. It was the last thing she had expected to see. An enclosure with a kitten in it. No, several kittens. They came out from behind an elaborate scratching post, tumbling into each other and scampering off, only to dash back moments later, ready for another tumble.

One particular ginger kitten caught Ronnie's attention. It was the most playful of the bunch, and most vocal, mewing as it leaped from one spot to another, and doing the most comical acrobatics.

Ronnie laughed. Its fur was just about the same color as Red's hair. And as it came closer, she noticed its eyes were blue-green, also like his. Maybe *he* should buy this kitten. They would be a perfect match.

No. *She* should buy it. Andy had asked her for a pet while he was at SickKids, but there was no way she could have dealt with such a responsibility at that time. But now things were different. Andy was back home, and taking care of a kitten would be manageable. He would love it. It would be the best surprise she could think of for his birthday...

But how could she keep it a secret till then? A sudden idea popped in her head. She could ask Red if he could take care of it until Andy's birthday. It was a long shot, but she could try...

With excitement swirling in her veins, she strode over to a staff member. She was going to do this! "Ginger" was coming home with her. After lunch.

Red's meeting with the Australian magnate had gone longer than expected, but with superlative results. All of his projected outcomes of the meeting had been achieved. And more. His legal team had been present to see to the technical details of the contract, and after heartily shaking the magnate's hand and wishing him a good flight back to Australia, Red had left the meeting, elated at having secured this new project for his Melbourne office, a world-class art gallery with specialty restaurants, gift shops and teaching studios.

Red placed the garment bag with his jeans and shirt in the back seat of the limo. Not wanting to keep Ronnie waiting, he had decided not to change. He instructed Liam to head to the CN Tower as the gold stylized letters of Brannigan Architects International receded in the rearview mirror.

He was ready to celebrate, and he was looking forward to celebrating with Ronnie.

She was waiting just outside the main entrance. After exchanging greetings and the news that their respective meetings had gone well, they proceeded into the building and reached the glass-fronted elevator that would take them up the iconic tower to 360, the restaurant 1150 feet above ground that revolved every seventy-two minutes. But first, Red wanted Ronnie to experience the first view of the city at the LookOut. As they rocketed upward amid gasps and a few excited shrieks, Ronnie did what many did the first time in the tower: instinctively move away from the glass panel as the elevator shot up. It was packed, and as she stepped back, one foot landed on Red's shoe and she faltered, her body pressing against him. Red's arms instinctively encircled her waist, and the rest of the visitors in the elevator disappeared as his mind and body registered only the sensory impact of Ronnie in the tight circle of his arms.

And then he promptly dropped them as Ronnie gained her balance. The door opened and the visitors surged toward the floor-to-ceiling window walls, while others ventured to the glass floor, showing the dizzying vertical view.

Red was glad it was sunny, so Ronnie could have the experience of enjoying a magnificent view of the cityscape. She was leaning toward one window with an expression of childlike awe, and the thought suddenly occurred to him that her son should have this experience also. He saw her reaching up to clasp her locket wistfully before turning to face Red. "I will definitely have to return with Andy," she declared. "He'd love it!"

"He's not afraid of heights?"

Ronnie laughed. "My little guy isn't afraid of much. He's tougher than he looks." Suddenly she unclasped her locket and opened it before handing it to Red. "The origin of Andrew is Greek, *Andreas*, and it means strong, courageous, brave. That's him," she said, her voice softening.

Red gazed at the photo. It was tiny, but he could see the resemblance to Ronnie. "He obviously takes after you," he murmured, handing it back to her.

She snapped it shut and put it back on. "I don't always feel strong and courageous."

"I don't think you give yourself enough credit," he shot back. "But I was actually referring to his looks. He's a cute kid."

Seeing the emotions play on her face, Red suddenly regretted his comments. He was venturing into sensitive territory for both Ronnie and himself, and should not have given Ronnie the opening to talk about her son, let alone offer an opinion about her. And letting his tongue slip about Andy resembling her was even worse.

He turned sharply away from her as she opened her mouth to respond. He felt like a heel, but he wanted to keep things between them as neutral as possible, and discussing her son, or making inferences about how he felt about her appearance, was only going to complicate things.

As Ronnie moved stiffly past him to navigate her way around the LookOut, Red suspected she had felt rebuffed. He saw her proceed to the glass floor and tentatively step onto it, and then his memory flooded with the image of Marco doing the same thing a year and a half earlier. A pang ripped through him, and as Ronnie turned to rejoin him, he forced himself to repress the memory and paste a smile on his face. There was no reason why he couldn't be civil during their time here. And even friendly without crossing personal lines. "Are you ready for the Sky Terrace next?" It was outdoors, one level below, still a refreshing one thousand plus feet above the ground.

"Uh...*no*! I'm quite fine inside, thank you," Ronnie replied. "I think I'd like to just sit for a while."

"So I guess the Edge Walk is out of the question also?"

Her wide-eyed response indicated she knew of the CN Tower's most extreme attraction: the world's highest hands-free external walk around the tower on a ledge five feet wide, situated even higher than the restaurant, 116 stories above the ground. The most daring visitors would be attached to an overhead safety rail by means of a trolley and harness system and walk around the tower in groups of six.

"Okay, lunch it is," he said, nodding. "I don't think I'm quite up to circumnavigating the tower in the middle of winter either."

Minutes later they were seated at a table in 360 The Restaurant. Ronnie had preferred it over a booth, so she could enjoy the view even more.

"Do you know that the CN Tower has the distinction of holding the Guinness World Record as the World's Highest Wine Cellar? So how about a glass?" Red suggested a white from the Niagara Peninsula and waited for Ronnie to approve before he nodded to the waitress.

His gaze couldn't help taking in the gray woollen dress Ronnie was wearing. It fit her body perfectly, and her ruby red lipstick matched the short coat she had just removed and placed over her chair.

After ordering, Red lifted his wineglass. "Cheers for us both having had a successful meeting."

She hesitated, eyeing him warily for a brief moment before nodding and clinking glasses. She took a sip. "Yes, I have good news for Casson."

"And we are going to have a fabulous lunch to celebrate getting what we wanted today…"

Ronnie's eyebrows arched. "This *is* a treat,"

she said, with a wave of her hand. "And I did manage to find something special for my son." She had another sip of her wine. I *was* going to get around to telling you about it," she murmured, her cheeks flushing, "especially since we'll be traveling back with you..."

"We?" Red frowned.

Ronnie bit her lip. "I couldn't help it. She was so sweet. And I know Andy will absolutely love her..." She gave Red a tentative smile. "I have to go pick her up after lunch..."

"Pick up who?"

"Ginger."

"Ginger?"

Ronnie nodded. "Our new...kitten," she said, breaking into a grin.

CHAPTER FIFTEEN

RED'S BLUE-GREEN EYES seemed to match the slate gray of his suit. He leaned forward, his brows furrowing, and Ronnie couldn't help thinking how distractingly handsome he was, with that black shirt and burgundy silk tie—

His frown dissolved. "Okay, I've heard of impulsive shopping, but this is…" He laughed.

"I hope you don't mind me bringing it back with us in the limo… You're not allergic to cats, are you?"

He waited until the waitress set down their plates, thanked her and gave Ronnie a bemused look. "No on both counts," he said. "I had a cat when I was a kid. He was round and orange, so I named him Pumpkin."

"Cute. Same as Ginger. She's got the most adorable coloring…" Ronnie smiled, her gaze shifting to Red's hair, and when she looked across at him, she realized he had noticed.

"Are you thinking Ginger and I might be related?" he said, eyes narrowing. "I don't have any kids, feline or otherwise, and I intend to keep it that way."

Ronnie's smile froze momentarily before fading. So Red Brannigan II didn't want kids. Was it because the responsibility would interfere with his jet-setting lifestyle, or was it simply because he was too self-centered and enjoyed freedom and relationships with no ties? Her gaze flitted over him. He was smart, handsome—no, damn handsome— and wealthy, but whoever ended up with him would have to be happy to have him alone, with no little Reds to carry on the Brannigan lineage...

Not everybody had a paternal or maternal instinct...

"So you're okay with this?" she said brusquely. "Me bringing Ginger back in the limo?"

"I'm not an unreasonable guy," he said, smirking. "I'm sure the three of us can get along in the close confines of the limo for a couple of hours..." His mouth curved into a smile, and Ronnie caught a flash of a dimple in one cheek. She reached for her glass of water, suddenly feeling too warm, and decided to delay her proposal to have him keep

Ginger temporarily until they were back on the road. She surveyed the sweeping view again. "I can only imagine how stunning the view must be at night, with the city all lit up…" she said, changing the subject.

"Would you live here?" Red said, eyeing her intently.

"I… I'm more of a small-town girl. Living in Parry Sound works perfectly for me and Andy, especially since I have family there. But I do like Toronto… I'll be traveling here more often once my new position officially begins."

"Well then, you'll be able to return to 360 for a night view…" He lifted and swirled his wineglass, the movement of the wine almost as hypnotizing as the laser gleam in the ocean-like depths of his eyes…

Would she return by herself? It would be bittersweet, enjoying the dazzling lights of the city while dining alone. Like watching a midnight indigo sky studded with stars, and having nobody to share the magic of it.

But you didn't want another man in your life… Her inner voice was right. Until a few days ago, she hadn't had time to think about sharing her life with anybody other than Andy.

And then a spinout in bad weather had

forced her to share space and time with Red. She blinked with the sudden awareness that there was a puzzle piece missing in her life, an empty space that had gone unnoticed during Andy's health crisis.

Ronnie had put her entire focus on Andy's treatment and recovery. She had had little time to think about or worry about anything or anybody else, including herself.

You have time now...

"Do we have time for a coffee? Dessert?"

Ronnie was jolted out of her thoughts. Those eyes fixed intently on her sent her emotions into a spin. "I'm fine," she said. "The desserts look amazing, but I couldn't eat one more thing."

"Next time, then." He nodded, a glitter in his eyes. "You're probably anxious for us to pick up the new addition…"

"Oh, are you new parents?" The waitress arrived at their table. "I couldn't help overhearing. How wonderful!" she gushed. "Is it a he or a she?"

"A she," Red answered before Ronnie could correct the waitress.

"How lovely. Girls are special."

"Very." Red smiled as he looked straight at Ronnie.

"What's her name?"

"Ginger." Red was grinning now, his gaze flicking from the waitress to Ronnie.

"Aww. Does she have hair like her daddy?"

"She does, indeed," Red chuckled.

"She must be a pretty little thing, if she takes after both of you! Congratulations!"

"Thank you," he said, taking the credit machine from her. "And lunch was excellent."

Ronnie was speechless, embarrassed and self-conscious that Red would let the waitress think that they were married and new parents.

"I can't believe you just did that," she said when the waitress was out of earshot.

Red just laughed and stood up. He walked around and leaned forward to pull out Ronnie's chair as she got up. "Shall we go? But before we fetch our little darling, would you mind if we make one stop?"

Red hadn't intended to check out Brannigan Architects International's latest accomplishment during this visit, but something made him want to show Ronnie the luxury condo residence he had designed and would be moving into at the end of the month. He had decided that it was time to move out of the condo his parents had gifted him, and into one of the penthouse suites of the residence. They didn't mind; they told him they'd be happy to keep it for out-of-town friends and guests who came to visit them.

Red suppressed a cynical laugh. His parents were hardly ever back in Toronto; they were too busy traipsing all over the world. He had accepted their perennial absence for the most part; when it did irk him, he repeated his vow to himself that unlike them, he would be very present in his future child or children's lives…

The residence, which he had named the Four-Leaf Clover to honor his Irish heritage, was a decadent Harbourfront development that was actually shaped like a clover, with each of the four circular leaf sections boasting floor-to-ceiling windows, and rooftops surfaced with green solar lights that illuminated at night. The opulent entrance, designed to represent the stem of the plant, had a massive Canadian maple-leaf-shaped double door of Waterford crystal that opened to a luxurious marble foyer with Waterford chandeliers. The residence, scheduled to officially open at month's end, included two gourmet restaurants that would feature Canadian and international cuisine, and an authentic Irish pub.

Red had designed the sprawling suites with high-end features: hardwood floors, vaulted ceilings and private terraces with spectacular views of the city and harbor. The amenities that residents could enjoy were those that Red appreciated himself: infinity pools, a state-of-the-art gym, a conference suite and library, and a meditation room.

The official opening would take place a week after the grand opening of Franklin's Resort, and Red felt a surge of excitement at the thought of starting a new chapter in his life with the move.

Red had told Ronnie about the residence, and that he wanted to have a quick glance before returning for the grand opening, but he hadn't revealed that he was the principal designer, and that he would be moving into one of the penthouse suites. As he pressed a special code to enter the building and walked through the grand foyer, Ronnie's wide-eyed expression gave him a tingling pleasure that superseded his previous sense of satisfaction with his accomplishment.

"Wow," she said, her gaze flying between the chandeliers and the opulent decor. "I've never been in a place like this..."

Something in her tone caused a strange twinge in his chest as she preceded him into the gleaming brass and marble elevator. As Red took her on a tour of the pool room, gym, conference and meditation rooms, she sporadically commented on the choice of colors, styles, floor coverings and features of each room, nodding her approval. It was the library that rendered her speechless for a few moments. She pivoted to take in the floor-to-ceiling bookshelves already stacked with new books, the luxurious high-back armchairs and recliners, and shot Red an appreciative grin.

"Whoever designed this is my kind of designer," she murmured, swirling around again to take it all in.

"And mine," he said, chuckling. "Are you ready to continue skyward? You've been in the CN Tower. I'd like to show you another spectacular view."

Ronnie's eyebrows lifted. "Why not? I doubt I'll get this chance again."

As they returned to the elevator, Red thought about Ronnie's words. They had been uttered without bitterness or longing. She had simply stated a fact that she believed to be true, a fact she accepted with calm practicality.

This was a side of a woman he was unfamiliar with. Sofia had grown up having and expecting luxury and extravagance in her life. It had become obvious to Red that she was never satisfied. The more she had, the more she wanted.

That was not the kind of woman *he* wanted in his life… and sooner or later, he would have realized that, if she had not broken up with him first.

As the doors opened to the penthouse level, Red ushered Ronnie toward his suite. While he had been settling into the estate in Parry Sound, his personal administrative assistant had arranged for the new furnishings to be delivered here and arranged where Red had specified. She had also arranged for his personal belongings to be transferred from his previous condo to this one, unpacked and put in their assigned places. He had only to walk in and enjoy life in his new penthouse.

Red was looking forward to checking it out…

He was not disappointed. As he scanned the sprawling open-concept space, Red nodded in satisfaction at the gleaming European kitchen, the sleek, Northern Italian furnishings in the living area, the heated hardwood floors, exotic area rugs and the eclectic decor. Perfect. Minimalistic but not stark. Comfortable. He turned to Ronnie. "Comments?"

"Stunning. Sleek and elegant, but not stuffy." She walked to the nearest floor-to-ceiling window. "Breathtaking view…" She stared out at the cityscape and the impressive view of the CN Tower. "Awesome."

Red joined her, and for a few moments they looked out together. He had chosen this suite for its spectacular positioning and iconic views.

"Come out on the terrace," he murmured.

Ronnie followed him past a spacious bedroom and as she took a few steps forward onto the terrace and looked down at the dizzying view, she suddenly swayed. Red reached out to help her steady herself.

"It's a different sensation, being out here, as opposed to looking out the window," she said apologetically, inhaling deeply. "I'm feeling a little light-headed."

Red steered her inside. He led her into the nearest room and had her sit down on an upholstered bench at the end of the king-size bed. He sat next to her and looked at her closely. "Are you feeling dizzy now? Light-headed still? Close your eyes and tilt your head forward."

She closed her eyes and when she swayed away from him, Red's arm shot out to stop her. He moved her gently back against him and kept his hand clasped around his arm. "Okay, take a deep breath," he murmured close to her ear. "Nice and slow. And let it out…"

As she inhaled, her head came up and his lips brushed against her temple, igniting a thudding in his chest. Her skin was so soft and rose-scented, and Red instinctively felt the urge to kiss her.

Don't...

Ronnie turned her head and opened her eyes at that moment. Those bright chestnut eyes with the soft fluttering of her eyelashes were his undoing...

CHAPTER SIXTEEN

RONNIE BLINKED, DISORIENTED. Red's arm was around her, holding her as if he were afraid she would fall off the seat, and he was looking at her in a way she had not seen before. Was it concern? The intensity of the fathomless depths of his eyes sent a shiver through her. If she didn't know any better, she'd think it was more than just concern. Tenderness, maybe…

She could still feel his breath fanning her cheek, and the sudden swell of his chest as he inhaled deeply himself. Her heart did a pirouette, followed by a tap dance across her chest. She couldn't deny that she liked the feel of Red against her, the protective clasp of his hand on her arm, the red-gold hair and scruff she'd be tempted to reach up and touch…if they were more than just acquaintances.

"Are you okay, Ronnie?"

His voice was husky, and the way her name

tumbled out of his mouth so easily made her pulse leap. "Um… I'm fine now. I'm okay with heights…but it's a whole different feeling when you're actually *outside*."

Ronnie saw Red's mouth quirk at her choice of words. And couldn't stop staring at his lips. She felt her stomach muscles contracting. A sensation of desire swept through her, and as she gazed upward at him, her cheeks burning, she could tell that Red was all too aware of her state of being. His hand slipped from her arm to cup her head gently as he leaned down to grant her unspoken request.

The gentle pressure of Red's lips on hers galvanized her. Ronnie's arms moved of their own accord around his neck. She felt herself sinking into a wonderland, her body drifting into the depths of pleasure…a pleasure she had believed herself to be immune to.

If she had been light-headed moments earlier, now her whole being felt as if it were in a no-gravity universe, with nothing but the pull of desire between her and Red…

She was floating on clouds…

And then the clouds darkened. She wasn't dealing with reality.

She pulled away from Red and she met his questioning gaze, trying to unravel her jumbled thoughts.

What was she doing? She was totally out of her element. Red was single, free and had said he didn't want kids, or something to that effect. So he was obviously just attracted to her physically.

But it wouldn't be right to encourage that attraction, or succumb to it. There was too much at stake. She had a kid, and playing around with a multimillionaire bachelor whose lifestyle was totally different from hers was not something she could allow herself to do. Her first priority had always been Andy... and she had no intention of doing anything that would change that. Even a little.

She stood up and raised her chin, shooting him a frosty look. "Let's forget what just happened." As she strode to the glass doors, she glanced back, adding, "Being this high up must have depleted the oxygen to my brain."

Making me lose my common sense and respond to your kiss, she added silently.

The limo stopped at the Eaton Centre. "I'd better come with you," Red said, and leaped out before Ronnie could reply.

"I'm pretty sure I can handle this by myself," she said, once he had come around to where she stood.

"I'll be there to make sure that you don't

get all soft when you see those little fur balls, and decide to adopt more than one. I wouldn't want to have too many feline claws ready to strike in the limo," he added with a smirk.

Ronnie raised an eyebrow but chose not to reply. He followed her quickened pace with a leisurely stride, occasionally sweeping an appreciative gaze over her. She seemed not to notice the heads that turned to glance at her...

Minutes later they were watching the antics of half a dozen kittens in the enclosure. "That's her!" Ronnie said excitedly, pointing to a kitten that had pounced on a sibling and then scampered away with a triumphant meow.

"How can you tell?" Red frowned. "They all look the same to me. But maybe you should pick out a kitten with a more subdued character." He pointed. "Look, she's tormenting her other sister. Or brother. Maybe you should consider changing her name from Ginger to Tiger."

"A mother can always pick out her own," she retorted. "And I want a kitten with a little spunk. She'll be great with Andy."

"Ah, I see there has already been some bonding," he chuckled. "Okay, Mama, is there anything else you need to pick up before we head back? A carrier, food, litter box, protective gloves, face guard?"

Her jaw dropped. "Really?" She rolled her eyes. "It's all taken care of and put aside for me. I paid earlier. I just need to get Ginger." She waved over an employee, who reached for a carrier and a leash behind the counter and headed their way.

"Aw, are you Ginger's daddy?" The employee grinned as he approached. His gaze shifted to Red's hair. "Looks like you're the perfect match!"

"Indeed," Red replied dryly. "I just hope she takes to me as well as she took to her mama here…"

Red was relieved that they had left the midafternoon city congestion and were now just past Barrie on the 400 North, heading back to Parry Sound. A little over an hour to go. Ginger had initially expressed her displeasure at her new confinement, mewing incessantly for the first half hour, but was now napping.

Since they had left the penthouse, and for the last hour, Ronnie had been quiet—actually, more like aloof—and had directed most of her communications to the kitten, which she had finally released from her carrier and snuggled in her arms, murmuring to her as she stroked Ginger's fur. And after Ginger had fallen asleep, Ronnie had avoided his gaze, preferring to look out the window, when not glancing down at the puff of orange in her arms.

Ronnie was obviously not happy that he had kissed her. And maybe she was upset at herself for having responded.

He should be upset, too. Kissing Ronnie had been an impulsive and dumb thing to do.

Exciting, yes; it had ignited a flame that had begun to sizzle through his nerve endings in the most provocative way...but still dumb.

Although the silence was awkward, he decided it was best to try to focus on something else. He snapped open his briefcase, and at that moment Ginger woke up with a plaintive meow. And wouldn't stop.

"Okay, Mama, can you do something to pacify your little one? I'm sure she'll sense your motherly empathy and experience and settle down." His brows furrowed. "I don't know if I can take this the whole way back home."

"I suppose I could try to give her some milk from the carton I bought," Ronnie said coolly.

"Well, do whatever you think will work," he drawled. "Or I'll be needing a drink from the minibar. Or two."

"I can understand why you wouldn't want kids," she said, not bothering to conceal her disapproval. "It takes a lot of patience to be a parent."

His frown deepened. He had no intention of getting into a conversation about kids. Or parenting. "That's why you're adopting the kitten and I'm not," he said lightly. "And hopefully she'll get used to your place quickly and not keep you up during the night…"

Ronnie blinked at him but didn't reply. She put Ginger back in the pet carrier and reached for the carton and bowl from one of the bags on the floor beside her. She poured a small amount of milk in the bowl and carefully un-latched the carrier. "Well, hello again, little darling," she crooned, stroking the kitten's head and back. "No need to fuss. Drink your milk and we'll be home soon…"

Red felt something flicker in his chest at the tender scene. Despite the current friction in the air between them, he couldn't help thinking again that Andy was a lucky lit-tle boy to have her as a mother. Getting him this kitten for his birthday was sure to add to Ronnie's responsibilities, especially with the new job she would be starting soon, yet she had seized the opportunity to get him this special gift, knowing it would bring her son happiness.

What puzzled him, though, was her assumption that he didn't want kids...and then, while he watched Ginger slurping up the milk, he recalled the comment he had made in the restaurant, about not having kids or cats and intending to keep it that way...

He hadn't added "for now" at the end of his statement...

That explained her judgmental and disapproving opinion of him, but Red couldn't attempt to change what she thought of him without going into explanations about his past, and that wasn't going to happen.

"Speaking of home..."

Red started and turned to see Ronnie's dark eyes fixed intently on him. She was biting her lip and her brow was creased, as if pondering whether she should go on.

"My home or yours?"

"That is the question," she said, stroking Ginger, who was now back in her arms and purring. "I have something I need to ask of you, and I know it might seem a little presumptuous, but I really want everything to be perfect for my son's birthday, um...and so, I need to ask you for a favor, just for a few days. Two, or maybe two and a half at the most. I'd be eternally grateful and it would just make the surprise even better—"

"What can I do for you, Ronnie?" he said dryly. Her previously cool tone was now sounding more civil. And maybe even a little humble.

"Would…would you be willing to keep Ginger at your place until Andy's birthday? He's back tomorrow and his birthday is the day after. I want to keep it an absolute surprise. I'd really appreciate it. And I'd pop by a few times to take care of the litter box…"

Red stared at her, stunned. This was the last thing he had expected to hear from her. "I'm not used to having a pet in the house," he said slowly. "I haven't taken care of a kitten since I was ten. I might forget to feed it or something."

"You can just leave the food out for her."

"Um…" He glanced away.

Liam turned on the windshield wipers as big snowflakes started coming down. Red turned back to Ronnie. "Have you considered offering this…exciting prospect…to your cousin?" He couldn't keep a slight note of sarcasm out of his voice.

"I actually had, but Andy would want to go see his little cousin right away when he gets home. And I don't want him to see Gin-

ger until his actual birthday." Her dark eyes
held an anticipatory gleam.

"Right." He pursed his lips. "Way to pull
on my heartstrings, Forrester, although it
sounded like you didn't think I had a heart
when it came to kids and kittens…"

"You're putting words in my mouth," she
murmured defensively. She shifted in her seat,
and the movement caused Ginger to slip out
of Ronnie's grasp. The kitten jumped across
onto Red's lap and crawled upward, rubbing
her face against his. Ronnie pulled her away
and cringed when Ginger's claws dug into the
fabric of his suit jacket. She extricated the kitten and looked ruefully at Red. "Sorry. She's
just doing what kittens do…"

"Right." He indicated the decreased visi-
bility ahead. "It's a good thing we're almost
home. I don't think the snow is going to let up."

"And speaking of home…" Ronnie's brows
lifted hopefully.

Red let out a big, dramatic sigh. "Fine, I'll
take her home."

"Aw, thank you! I'll think of some way to
repay you…"

"Just be on standby in case I need you," he
warned. "Especially if she starts crying in the
night. I need my beauty sleep…"

CHAPTER SEVENTEEN

RONNIE FELT A surge of happiness at Red's words. And an acceleration of her heartbeat. She couldn't remember when she had last felt so happy or excited, other than when she had heard the wonderful news about Andy's remission.

She gazed at Red's profile as he looked away to focus on the road as Liam drove through a particularly snowy stretch.

He had a strong, firm jaw and features that she was sure had caused a spike in more than one woman's pulse… And he did have a kind heart, she admitted grudgingly to herself. Who else would have agreed to keep a kitten for someone they had just met a couple of days earlier?

Ronnie placed Ginger back into the carrier when they approached the exit that would take them into Parry Sound. Snow was falling at a much gentler rate than the almost white-out conditions around Barrie. She shivered and hoped that Red would start the fire while they set up Ginger's corner…

The thought gave her a jolt. It had sounded like a statement someone might have made if they had been married or living together. And the image it suddenly triggered in Ronnie's mind made her blush. How ridiculous to picture herself cradling Ginger, snuggled under a cozy throw that Red had placed over her shoulders.

Okay, this has to stop. Just because Red agreed to keep Ginger for a couple of days didn't mean he had any domestic inclinations where *she* was concerned…

But would you like there to be? a rogue inner voice pressed her.

Ronnie stole another glance at Red. He had looked mighty fine in a cardigan and jeans, but in that tailored suit… Her gaze slipped from his broad chest to the way his long legs filled out his trousers and an undeniable shiver went through her.

Maybe there *was* something going on. In *her*, anyway.

The snowflakes were coming down soft and wet when they arrived at Red's place. Red thanked Liam and wished him a good night before jumping out to get Ronnie's door. She handed him the carrier and stepped out carefully. Red motioned for her to precede him and once inside the house, he invited her to join him in the salon. "The first order of business when I get in is to get the fire going," he said brusquely. "And then I need to insist on a transition period for Ginger before I let you go home…"

"What…do you mean?" Ronnie said, her brow wrinkling.

Ginger began to meow in her carrier, which he had set down on one of the recliners. He gestured toward it. "I have to make sure Ginger is happy here. So after I start up the fire, you can get her litter box set up and let her out of her carrier while I boil some water for tea. See how she takes to her temporary digs. And if she shows me a reasonable amount of love—and doesn't tear my place apart—I'll be happy to keep her."

"You didn't tell me there would be conditions," she protested, shooting him an accusing look. "I thought her staying with you for a couple of days was a done deal."

Red gazed at her for a long, worrisome moment. She couldn't believe that he had first said yes, only to now reveal that things might not work out after all…

"It is," he said, grinning. "I just couldn't resist teasing you."

* * *

Red was acutely aware of Ronnie shuffling about, setting up Ginger's food and water dishes. He felt warm and rolled up his sleeves, but he suspected that it had little to do with the fire. The warmth was inside him. Despite the warning voice telling him he should remain detached, he knew deep down that he liked having Ronnie around. In his house, in his truck, on his pond. In a restaurant. Sleeping by the fire...

Maybe "liked" wasn't the right word...

A couple of glances over his shoulder as he arranged the kindling on top of the logs in the grate revealed Ronnie preparing the litter box and placing it in a corner behind a large potted plant. He heard Ginger's contented purring as she lifted her out of the carrier and set her down in the litter box. When the fire was robust, Red drew the panels of the safety screen together and stood up. He walked over to where Ronnie was and they both watched as the kitten leaped over to the area rug, surveying her new surroundings and emitting a few plaintive mews.

He and Ronnie exchanged bemused glances, and he couldn't help thinking how natural it felt to be doing this with her. Watching their new kitten together.

Whoa. *Her* new kitten.

"Oh, look, Red!" Ronnie clasped his forearm. "She's rolling like a little ball. Oh, my gosh, she's so cute!" And then she let go to kneel down on the rug beside Ginger.

Red watched her playing with the kitten, his pulse elevated from the brief touch of her fingers on his arm. He smiled at Ginger's antics and at Ronnie speaking to the kitten as if she were a child, and stroking her after each roll or tumble. In the background, he could hear the intermittent crackling of the fire.

Anybody looking in on them would think they were a happy family...

That's all he had ever wanted growing up... to do normal things with his parents, like the other kids in his class and in his neighborhood. Simple things.

Things that Ronnie probably did with Andy...

And things that he could imagine himself doing one day. With his own kid...

CHAPTER EIGHTEEN

Clasping Red's forearm had been involuntary. It had happened before she could even think about stopping herself. The feel of his bare arm under her hand had instantly restored her awareness, though, and she had casually let go and knelt on the carpet with Ginger, making sure that her flaming cheeks were not in Red's line of vision.

Ronnie watched Ginger as she then ambled toward the pet bed that Ronnie had placed a comfortable distance from the fireplace. The kitten sniffed curiously around it and explored other nooks and crannies around the room before returning to curl up in it. Ronnie cheered inwardly and as Red excused himself to go to the kitchen, she sat down on one of the recliners. She would leave after a quick text to Casson.

She was happy to hear that the baby's fever had gone down, and Justine was feeling better. Relieved, Ronnie texted that she'd be over in the morning to share the details of the business meeting with him. A glance toward the cat bed made Ronnie set down her cell phone quickly. Ginger was gone. A quick scan of the room showed no sign of her.

She had to find her. Ginger could get into anything in such a huge place and ingest something that could be harmful... Her heart drumming, Ronnie dashed into the kitchen, breathlessly told Red that she was looking for Ginger, and dashed out again. The doors down the foyer were all closed so she headed to the carpeted stairway. Ginger was small, but she could have managed the trek upstairs.

Ronnie's dismay grew as she inspected the first two rooms and found no sign of Ginger. And no luck in the room she had occupied her first night in the mansion. She entered the open double doors of the room opposite that one, and with a jolt realized she was in the master bedroom. *Red's room.*

She had never seen such a huge room. It incorporated a living space with an amber leather couch and chair. The king-size bed with what she realized, as she stepped closer, was a live-edge slate headboard. The floor was a gleaming expanse of dark hardwood. The entire wall behind the bed consisted of floor-to-ceiling window panels, providing a view of the pond and a majestic stretch of snow-dusted pines. Two of the side panels were actually doors leading to a balcony jutting out in a spacious half-circle.

As she turned away from the view, her gaze fell on a photo frame on the night table near her. Someone had taken a photo of Red and a little boy, probably four or five years old. They were both wearing Toronto Maple Leafs caps and were sitting in a stadium. They had smiles on their faces and were making a thumbs-up sign. Ronnie's heart skipped a beat. Was this cute little boy with the ruddy cheeks and dark brown eyes related to Red? A nephew, perhaps?

She knew next to nothing about Red.

Perhaps he was separated or divorced... The thought created a funny swirl in her stomach, but she would have to process her feelings later. She needed to find Ginger.

A ripple of the bed skirt caught her eye. And then the unmistakable flash of a ginger-colored tail. Ronnie quickly turned around to close the double doors before crouching by the edge of the bed, calling Ginger's name softly. A responding meow followed, along with the appearance of Ginger's little face. Ronnie lunged forward to scoop her up, but lost her balance in the process, and she found herself sprawled on the bedside floor mat, kitten in both hands.

And then her gaze flew to the doors as they clicked open, Red framed in the center, a crooked smile on his face.

The last thing Red had expected to find was Ronnie lying flat on the floor next to his bed, holding Ginger.

After she had run in and out of the kitchen, he had turned off the boiling kettle and then gone upstairs to join in the search. The closed double doors had puzzled him and he had reopened them, doubting his memory. And there they both were, on the floor.

He strode over to Ronnie and offered her a hand to assist her in getting up, but instead, she handed him the kitten. She shifted awkwardly to right herself, her cheeks flushed. "I'm sorry. This little rascal was under your bed."

"Don't be sorry," he said with a chuckle. He lifted Ginger in front of his face. "It's this little rascal who should apologize." The kitten meowed and licked his chin. "Now don't try to sweet talk me, Miss Ginger." Red caught Ronnie's eye. "I think she's trying to tell me she'd rather sleep with me in my nice big bed instead of her teensy one. Not a chance."

Ronnie's eyebrows lifted. "Well, you might

want to put her bed in a corner of your room. You could keep a better eye on her."

"What?" He feigned a frown. "This was not in the original contract."

"She'll be lonely downstairs. And she'd wander," Ronnie said authoritatively, walking toward the door.

"I see." Red followed. "Why don't you just stay the night?" he said impulsively. "You can have your room back and she can sleep with *you*?"

Ronnie stared at him, blinking. "You're kidding, right?"

"I'm not. This way, we both get to sleep."

"Why do you think I wouldn't be able to sleep at my place?" Ronnie frowned.

"You'd be too worried about Ginger."

Ronnie shook her head and continued out the door and down the stairway. "I'm not at all worried," she said, turning on the last step to smile brightly at him. "I can see that Ginger is in very good hands."

He was losing all control, Red thought repeatedly as he followed Ronnie back downstairs. What inner sorcerer had made him ask Ronnie to stay? His invitation had slipped out of his mouth before his common sense could intervene...

He set Ginger down in her carrier as Ronnie watched. He straightened and looked at her curiously. "What time do you expect your son to be back tomorrow?"

Ronnie's face brightened as she clasped her locket. "Around noon. I can't wait." At the entrance, Ronnie slipped on her coat before Red could help her. She put on her boots and then turned to him. "Thanks again for doing this," she said, offering him a tentative smile. "Um, I… I hope you don't mind me asking…but I couldn't help noticing the photo of you and a little boy upstairs. Is he a relative?"

Red could feel the smile that had started to form freeze on his face. "He could have been," he replied brusquely.

"Oh." She shook her head, her forehead creasing. "I'm sorry; I shouldn't have asked—"

"His name is Marco. He's my ex-girlfriend's son." Red looked away. Just saying the words had precipitated an unexpected wave of emotion that hit him like a punch in the stomach. Only, instead of a fist, it was a jagged hunk of meteor, piercing him with all the feelings that he had experienced in the past year: sadness, bitterness, loss, helplessness. He glanced back at Ronnie, and another wave hit him when he saw the empathy in her eyes.

CHAPTER NINETEEN

RONNIE WISHED SHE hadn't brought up the photo. It had evoked painful memories for Red and she felt terrible, but she couldn't take the words back. She looked at him helplessly. It was strange to suddenly see a different side to him. And to catch the flicker of hurt in the depths of his eyes, as if invisible arrows had struck their exact target.

She pulled the collar of her coat. "Sorry it didn't work out for you."

He gave her a piercing stare, as if he were trying to decide whether he should say more.

"I'm not," he said finally.

Her eyebrows arched uncontrollably.

"I don't regret that it didn't work out with *her*. The hard part was that it meant I wouldn't be able to see her son anymore."

And Marco had meant the world to Red. It was in his eyes…

He turned to the fire. Kneeling on one knee, he placed another log on the grate.

Her heart suddenly swelled as she gazed at his broad back and stooped head. He was a guy with a sense of humor, but now she knew that there was also another part of him that he probably hid from most people. A part that hurt like hell.

She understood what hurting felt like. Especially these past two years. The cause of her pain was different to his, but pain was pain.

Right or wrong, she went over and reached for Red's hand and gently squeezed it. His body swiveled toward her, and in the firelight she could see his eyes had a misty sheen. Suddenly he had both her hands in his and he was pulling her to him. And she had no desire to pull away. In seconds she was kneeling on the mat with her head pressed against his chest and her arms around his waist, with his clasped around her back. His body was solid, warm, and felt...nice. *Very nice.*

Was that his heart drumming against her ear, or was it her pulse? She breathed in the scent of his cologne. Intoxicating. A warning light flickered in her brain, but she ignored it, wanting this rush that she was feeling to continue...

She lifted her face and at the brush of her jaw on his chin, he leaned down and a second later, his lips were on hers. They both froze at the initial impact, and then Ronnie felt the gentle pressure of Red's mouth inviting her to respond.

She wanted to. *Needed to.*

Ronnie closed her eyes, immersed in such waves of pleasure that she thought she was spinning, airborne. She thought she heard her phone buzzing, but she ignored it. Inside, a hunger was gnawing at her, a hunger that she never thought she'd feel…

Her heart was thumping so loudly that she had to take a breath. Red's lips trailed down her neck, each kiss activating a sizzle that radiated throughout her body.

His cheek descended farther, brushing against her locket.

And that was when common sense flooded her.

She stiffened and pulled back, forcing herself to ignore the flash of hurt in his eyes. She should have never allowed herself to get to this point. She rose and turned away from Red, trying to get her breathing back to normal.

But how could life ever be normal after tonight?

"I think—" she paused shakily "—that it's best if you stay away from women like me until you figure out a way of getting over your past relationship."

"I am over it," he rasped, also rising.

"Over *her*, maybe. But not over her son…" She bit her lip. "You need to let go… Because otherwise, I don't think you can move on." She stopped as his eyes narrowed, his expression fierce. A sudden thought came to her. Red was attracted to her but inevitably pulled away, and Ronnie could see now that Andy was probably the reason. How could Red even contemplate the idea of another child in a relationship, when he hadn't let go of Marco?

And perhaps there was even more to it than that…

She saw the muscles in his jaw flicking. He might not want or be ready to hear anything else, but she felt compelled to try.

"Red, can I just say something else? You mentioned that you were an only child, and that your parents had often been absent when you were young, traveling around the world." Ronnie paused as his gaze turned sharply to her. She bit a corner of her lip. "Have you ever thought that…that maybe you're not only still trying to heal from the loss of Marco, but also from the physical and emotional loss of your parents during much of your formative years?"

Something flickered in Red's eyes, and Ronnie knew her words had touched a nerve. He was still hurting…

Ronnie felt his ache in her own heart. Imagined what he must have felt as a child. He turned away.

"I think," she said softly behind him, "that accepting your loss doesn't mean you have to forget Marco. Or feel guilty that you might have caused him to feel hurt over the breakup…"

She saw his shoulders stiffen. "There are people…professionals who can help with any lingering feelings you might be experiencing…and losses that go farther back…"

Moments passed and Ronnie wondered if maybe she had said too much. "I'm sorry," she murmured.

Red slowly turned around to face her. "I never thought about it—all of it—in that way before…" He nodded slowly. "I might just see who I can talk to when I get back to Toronto. But what you said makes a lot of sense." He held her gaze for a few moments. "Thank you, Ronnie."

She nodded, and bit her lip. "It's a lot to deal with. Look, Ginger is sleeping. So if you don't mind, Red, I'd like to head back home. I'll just take a cab."

Red felt a lurch in his stomach muscles as he stared back at her. He didn't want her to leave. Moments ago, Ronnie had offered her perspective on a condition that had previously seemed hopeless to him. He had been struggling with the challenge of letting go of his recent past. He had accepted the end of his relationship with Sofia, and maybe even with Marco, but Red hadn't been able to stop thinking about him.

Accepting your loss doesn't mean you have to forget Marco.

No, he didn't have to try to forget Marco, he now realized with wonder. He could cherish the memories they had shared. His loss might still make him sad at times, but perhaps he could let go of his lingering feelings of guilt, and now move forward and allow a new relationship to develop…including one with a child.

And maybe Ronnie was right about his unresolved issues with his parents, and their connection to his loss of Marco…but he would deal with that later…

"No. *I'll* take you home."

But first he had to deal with what had happened between him and Ronnie earlier…

How had he ended up doing what he had vowed never to do? Kissing her like he had been stranded in a desert for weeks and she had just brought him water. He had to try to apologize. Red inhaled and exhaled deeply. "Look, Ronnie, I'm sorry if I made you uncomfortable earlier. It wasn't my intention."

She didn't respond.

"I'm sorry," he repeated. "I—I just got caught up in the moment... Can we just forget it happened?" What a stupid thing to say. How could he forget any of it? And it was the same request Ronnie had made after their kiss on his terrace...

She nodded slowly "I'm sorry, too." Minutes later, as he held the door of his truck open for Ronnie, Red caught a whiff of her perfume, a delicate rose fragrance that he had trailed along her neck and—

It was just beginning. The torture of remembering...

He turned on the radio to an easy listening channel. It would relieve them both of the effort to make small talk on the way to Winter's Haven...

Ronnie's phone buzzed, and he turned off the radio. He was able to hear the muffled voice of a man, but not the message.

"Oh, my God, Peter," Ronnie gasped. "Oh,

my God. Will he be okay? Are they doing tests? Does he have a concussion?"

Red felt his heart begin to thud. Something had happened to Andy...

He glanced at Ronnie. She was staring straight ahead, her face creased with worry. She listened intently to her ex-husband while blinking rapidly.

"I'm going home to get my car and I'm heading to Gravenhurst right away," she blurted while he was still talking. "My poor baby. Tell him I love him. I'll be there as soon as I can!"

A few seconds later she hung up and turned to Red. "Andy fell and hit his nose on the edge of the coffee table. It started to bleed and he also had a gash that needed stitches. They're doing more tests, given his health history." Alarm flickered in her dark eyes.

"Did Andy's father feel it was serious?"

"He said it was under control, but still, I should be there... What if there are complications?"

"It's late, and by the time you get there—it'll take you more than an hour in this weather—they might already have discharged him," he said gently. "Perhaps you should let Peter handle this. I'm sure he would let you know if there's a more serious issue." He activated the windshield wipers as the snow started up and then glanced over at Ronnie. "It's not the best weather to be traveling at night on the highway…"

"I could have been on my way already if I had answered my phone earlier." Her jaw clenched.

He frowned. When had her phone rung? Oh, yes…when they were—

"And he wouldn't have had to go through this ordeal by himself."

"He's not by himself, Ronnie; his dad is with him."

She waved a hand dismissively. "I shouldn't have been distracted. What if something worse had happened? I'd never forgive myself."

"It sounds like things are under control, and something like this could happen with or without you being there, Ronnie, so you don't have to beat yourself up over this," Red said in a nonjudgmental tone. "Kids fall, get stitches and need to go to the hospital."

"I think I have a little more experience with kids than you," she blurted. And then she shook her head. "I'm sorry. That was insensitive. I shouldn't have said that."

"Apology accepted. You're under stress."

Ronnie nodded. "Can you go a little faster?" She leaned forward, tapping nervously on the glove compartment.

"Ronnie, if you're that intent on driving to the hospital, I'm not letting you go alone." His tone was firm and her gaze shifted to him, her brows furrowed. "But the wisest thing to do—in *my* opinion—is to go home, wait for updates from Peter, and once he reassures you that Andy is fine—which I'm sure is the case—then you can go to sleep with peace of mind, and tomorrow Andy will be back in time for lunch and your hugs."

Red turned into Ronnie's driveway, and brought the truck to a stop near the doorstep. He switched off the wipers and in seconds the windshield was covered with a layer of snow. He swiveled in his seat to look Ronnie in the eye. "Why jeopardize your life by driving at night in these conditions? Andy needs you to stay safe…"

From the outdoor light that illuminated the interior of the truck, Red saw that Ronnie's initial glare had changed to a look of thoughtfulness as she weighed his words.

"Let Peter handle it," he murmured. "Let him be a dad…"

Ronnie stared out the window. She let out a long sigh. "Okay," she said, nodding slowly. "I'll call Peter. But if he calls back later and tells me I should go, I'll go…"

"Of course. And that's when you'll call *me*, and I'll pick you up and drive you there."

The drive back home was long, dark and lonely. When Red opened the front door, Ginger's mewing actually cheered him up. He opened up the carrier and lifted her out. She nuzzled his face and he stroked her head and back, marveling at how relaxing it felt.

He needed to relax. Think things through. Figure out how Ronnie Forrester had, in the three days since she had spun into his life, taken up residence in his mind.

Along with her son.

He hadn't wanted to complicate his life again by pursuing a relationship that involved a child.

But now…he was ready to open the door— if only a crack—to that possibility.

Ronnie had been very perceptive about the dynamics of his relationship with Marco. And something inside him had let go at her advice.

Lying in bed a little later, Red recalled the feel of Ronnie pressed against him and her response to his kiss that had sent ripples of desire through him. He could only imagine what might have transpired had she not pulled away…

CHAPTER TWENTY

RONNIE WAS ABOUT to put her finger on the snooze button and then remembered that Andy was coming home today. Peter had called shortly after Red had left last night, and said that Andy was fine and they would be heading home. Ronnie had changed into her pajamas and made herself a cup of chamomile tea, hoping it would settle the agitation in her stomach and chest caused not only by the initial worry over Andy but also by the ambivalent feelings churning up inside her over Red's embrace. And kiss.

But she couldn't just blame *him*.

She had started it, letting her empathy for his pain over Marco compel her to reach out and squeeze his hand. And then he had literally taken her breath away.

Unfortunately, the tea hadn't produced the results she had hoped for, and she had spent a good portion of the night shifting from side to side, while her thoughts kept turning to Red…

As she got out of bed, Ronnie reminded herself that she had Andy to think about. And she could not—*would not*—get involved with Red. No matter how much she was attracted to him.

She had no intention of trusting her deepest emotions to any man and then getting hurt if it didn't work out. More importantly, she didn't want Andy to get hurt.

Ronnie removed her locket before stepping into the shower. She really didn't have to worry that Red would be pursuing her. He had made it clear that he wanted them both to forget what had happened. And he obviously had trust issues, as well. His previous relationship hadn't worked out, and Ronnie didn't blame him for not wanting to repeat that kind of scenario with someone else.

So why, then, knowing all this, did she feel a twinge of hurt over his readiness to forget?

Red shut off his laptop and gazed at the ball of fur resting in her pet bed. Ginger had been surprisingly quiet during the night, so he couldn't blame the kitten for his lack of sleep. What had kept him awake were the images that kept popping up in his mind.

Dozens of images of Ronnie that circulated in his memory incessantly: her dazed look after spinning out; her peaceful expression while sleeping on the recliner; the breathtaking skate on the pond; the wonder on her face at the CN Tower; her pleasure as she watched Ginger's antics; and her luminous brown eyes that had seemed to melt into his when he had leaned forward to kiss her...

Declaring that he and Ronnie should just forget what had happened between them had been unrealistic. At least for *him*. She had seemed to have no problem agreeing that it would be best to forget.

He sighed. Why did thinking about Ronnie hurt?

Because you want her...

He blinked. He *did* want her. In his house and in his life.

Child and all.

It was time to stop living in the past. He had to accept that Marco had been a temporary gift in his life. Someone who had shown him that he had the capacity to love a child who wasn't biologically his and that he would be loved back. After considering what Ronnie had told him, Red knew it was time to accept the past and let go. He would never forget Marco, but he could move on and not feel guilty about it.

And now Red had the opportunity to accept and love another child simply because he was in love with the child's mother.

The realization shook him to the core. He didn't just *want* Ronnie; he was in love with her. He just had to come up with a way to make her feel the same way...

But would Ronnie trust him to stick around, even if times got tough? The stakes were high for her too, but he had to find a way to show her that he'd be there for the long run, through sunshine and storms. In sickness and in health. For both her and Andy.

There must be some way he could make her believe...

CHAPTER TWENTY-ONE

ANDY WAS FAST ASLEEP before Ronnie had finished the first song. Her heart swelled at the sight of his long, feathery lashes on his flushed cheeks. She was so glad to have him home. Earlier, when Andy had pulled open the dresser drawers to get a fresh set of pajamas, Ronnie's heartbeat had accelerated at the sight of his clothes arranged in neat piles. By Red. Knowing now that his past relationship had included the woman's child, for whom he had cared a great deal, Ronnie realized that going into Andy's room must have brought back some bittersweet memories...

And perhaps the reason Red had been ready to leave after that...

Ronnie's thoughts went back to the afternoon she and Andy had spent with Casson and Justine. They were perfect for each other, and they were so in love with their adorable baby. They deserved every happiness.

And so do you, her inner voice murmured.

Yes, she did. And she *was* happy. But she couldn't deny that there was a hollow in a corner of her heart, and wondered if it would ever be filled by love of a different kind...the love of a partner. A man whose love could encompass her son, as well. Without it, there would be no relationship.

But you didn't want a relationship...

Her inner voice was right. She hadn't wanted one after her marriage had ended, hadn't had time to even consider fitting another person in her life.

And now?

Now, nothing. Red Brannigan II had entered her life and there had been a mutual physical attraction between them, but he had clearly stated that they should forget what had happened. Ronnie put away her mug and got ready for bed, deliberately shifting her thoughts to Andy. She couldn't wait for his birthday tomorrow. He would be turning seven and celebrating with his family at home, unlike last year.

This birthday would be his best so far. He deserved it. Ronnie vowed that every birthday after that would be better than the last. This year, a kitten... What she needed to think about was whether she would go and pick up

Ginger, or if she should just call Red to see
if he could drop the kitten off at Casson's. If
she went with the latter, she could avoid seeing him.

Why did she feel so conflicted? She sighed.
Tomorrow was a big day and she hoped that,
unlike the night before, she'd be able to have
a decent sleep.

Without the memory of those blue-green
eyes and that red-hot kiss breaking into her
dreams.

Red had spent half the night at his laptop,
playing around with ideas for renovating the
mansion and developing some of the acreage.
And then some wild ideas had taken hold of
his imagination…

In the early hours of the morning, Red
had nodded off at the keyboard, and when
he had awoken, he had surveyed the design
templates he had created. Plans for all the
things a little boy would get excited about:
a water slide and pool; a basketball court; a
treehouse; and a mini movie theater. It was
crazy, and his plans might never be realized,
but he was going to wait for the right time to
show them to Ronnie…

Red knew very well that kids today liked
their electronics, but if they were like Marco,

they would enjoy all these activities, too. The thought had galvanized Red. It was the first time he had remembered something about Marco and felt happiness instead of grief. Happiness knowing he had played a positive part in the boy's life, at least for a while. He had shut down his laptop and gone to bed, knowing in his heart that he had come to a turning point. He had finally let go…

And maybe now a new chapter in his life could begin.

With a contentment he hadn't felt in a long time, Red felt himself drifting peacefully toward sleep.

CHAPTER TWENTY-TWO

RONNIE WOKE UP EARLY to a pink and baby blue sky. It promised to be a beautiful clear day. No snow, no freezing rain, just a whole lot of sunshine. Her little guy was seven today. And this was a birthday she hoped he would always remember.

Ronnie put her hair up in a ponytail and dressed quickly in jeans and a red T-shirt. After she made breakfast for Andy, she drove over to Casson and Justine's. Andy went off with Casson for a walk in the woods. Ronnie strode to the big living room window with its gorgeous view of the frozen bay and the section Casson had cleared off for skating. It immediately evoked the memory of Red sweeping her up and skating effortlessly around his pond, with her clasped tightly in his arms…

She was flooded with a longing that she never thought she'd feel again. But this longing was much stronger, perhaps because she knew it would not be fulfilled by the man who had caused it…

A man who had helped her make a giant step yesterday…to let go and not feel she had to be with Andy every waking moment, guarding him, protecting him from getting hurt, or being there when he was hurt. Red had made her realize that she had to relax and let Peter be a responsible parent too, without her hovering over them.

Red had taught her a lesson about trust.

She had to try to give up the reins of control and trust that Peter could do the job of looking after Andy as well as she had done. And even if he couldn't, she'd have to let go and hope that he would do the best he could.

Ronnie sighed. Red had given her a new perspective. Letting go was hard, though. But like it or not, she had to try. Perhaps now she could continue to let her guard down more, have more fun in her life, do things for herself.

And maybe the time would come when she'd be able to trust another man in her life…

The doorbell sounded. She strode to the door and when she opened it, her heart clanged at the sight of Red holding Ginger in her carrier.

She swallowed. "I—I thought… Casson told me *he'd* be driving over to pick her up…"

"I called him to say I could drop her off. He said he'd text you…"

Ronnie glanced across the room at her cell phone lying on the kitchen table where she had placed it upon arriving. Red stood on the doorstep, his eyebrows arching. "I'll get Ginger's bed in a minute… It's in the truck."

"Okay, thanks," Ronnie said, snapping out of her stupor. She set the carrier down in the foyer and watched as Red returned with the pet bed and a bag with the rest of the items for Ginger. Ronnie reached for the bed, but Red wasn't letting go. His brow was furrowed and he stood there blinking at her, with a steely intensity in his eyes. Eyes that seemed darker, the color of the stormy waters in some of the paintings of Georgian Bay by the Group of Seven.

"Ronnie, is there a chance we can talk before Andy's birthday?"

"Talk? Here?" Justine would be coming down with the baby at any moment…

"How about in my truck? We could go for a short ride, if you have time."

Ronnie's heart began drumming. "I—I'm going to bring Ginger upstairs and I—I have to let Justine know." She lifted the carrier and Red released his hold on the bed.

"Okay; I'll wait in the truck."

When Red saw her leaving the house a few minutes later, he jumped out to open the passenger-side door. "Okay if we just drive around the corner?" he said.

"Um, sure."

He drove out of Winter's Haven and down the highway. After a couple of minutes, he turned into a road through a densely wooded section that led to a small lake. He parked and then shifted in his seat to face her. She watched as he took a deep breath and exhaled slowly. "Ronnie, I can't forget…"

"What do you mean?" She knew exactly what he meant.

"You. I can't forget you." He rubbed his temple. "I didn't get much sleep last night. Or the night before." He let out a husky laugh. "In fact, you've kept me awake and thinking since you spun out before my eyes."

Ronnie felt her heart pulsing, trying to anticipate what he was going to say next. And how was she going to respond…

"I wasn't looking for anything like this to happen. I didn't think I was ready." He shrugged. "But it happened anyway."

Her heart was going to rocket right out of her chest. "Wh-what, exactly?"

He looked at her as if she were a student who just wasn't getting it. "I fell. Head. Over. Heels."

"For…?"

"For Ginger." At her stunned look, he added, "No, Ronnie. For *you*."

She blinked at the sudden tingling behind her eyelids, wanting to both laugh and cry.

"That has got to be the most original way to get yourself invited to a birthday party," she finally managed to say, trying to keep her voice steady.

It was Red's turn to look stunned. "That's all you can say?"

She wanted to climb over the truck's middle section and kiss him oh-so-thoroughly, but something in her resisted. "You could have just asked nicely for a piece of cake—"

He groaned and leaned toward her, cupping the back of her head while he kissed her. "I'll take this over a piece of cake any day," he murmured before his mouth closed over hers again.

Ronnie lost all sense of time and space. Red Brannigan II had ignited her appetite. And she wanted to have her fill.

She wrapped her arms around his neck.

Brought her hands to touch both sides of his face. Ran her fingers through his hair. And kissed him with a hunger that matched his.

Red looked deeply into Ronnie's eyes. This was what he had been waiting for. Everything he had gone through to get to this point had been worth it. He gently traced his fingers over the contours of her face. She was real. His feelings were real.

"We have to get back, Red."

Red traced the outline of her mouth. He loved the sound of his name on her lips.

"Okay," he murmured. "I'll be back later in time for cake…"

After dropping Ronnie off, Red headed to one of the malls. He couldn't very well show up empty-handed for Andy's birthday. He wished he had asked Ronnie what Andy might like. Halfway there, Red changed his mind. He had the perfect gifts for Andy at his place. *In Toronto.* He had intended to give them to Marco last year, but the breakup happened and he had shoved the items into a spare bedroom closet.

Andy was a Leafs fan, just like Marco. Red couldn't remember if it was Casson or Ronnie who had mentioned it, but it didn't matter. All that mattered was that he knew Andy would like the gifts. What kid wouldn't like an official hockey jersey of his favorite team? And a hockey stick signed by all the players? Red had bid on the latter at a charity event in Toronto and had triumphantly brought it home, excited to give it to Marco.

Red felt a twinge of sadness, but he knew in his heart that he had accepted his loss. Now he had the chance to give these gifts to a little boy who had no idea yet that Red loved his mother and wanted to start a new chapter of his life with her. And *him*.

He checked his watch. If he wanted to be back in time for the party, he'd have to leave now for Toronto. It would take a couple of hours there and back, depending on the traffic, but it would be worth it, seeing Andy's face when he opened up the gifts. Red approached the merging lane and put his foot on the accelerator, zooming onto the 400 South.

CHAPTER TWENTY-THREE

Ronnie was floating on air. She couldn't think of a better cliché for how she felt. But she wasn't ready to tell Justine about her and Red. Not yet. Today was about Andy, not her.

Casson and Andy hadn't returned from their walk. Ronnie told Justine about inviting Red to the party to thank him for keeping Ginger and then drove back to her cottage to change. She went to her room and looked through her closet. She hadn't chosen an outfit yet, and now, knowing that Red would be there, she wanted to pick something extra special.

Ronnie finally decided on a tailored burgundy dress with three-quarter-length sleeves. She liked its classic rounded neckline and below-the-knee straight skirt. She had bought it two years ago, but hadn't had the opportunity to wear it since. Until now. Her son's seventh birthday and Red's declaration warranted a celebration. A double celebration. And this was the perfect dress to celebrate in. She would wear it with black pantyhose and a low-heeled pair of pumps. And the only piece of jewelry she'd put on would be her locket.

Ronnie laid the dress on her bed and ran her palm over one of the sleeves. A delicious shiver skittered through her at the thought of Red running his hand over the fabric...with her in it.

She couldn't wait to see Red again. She wanted to sing, she was so happy. Whatever feelings she had had previously about not wanting or needing a man had dissipated when Red had revealed his feelings to her. And kissed her.

She had been afraid to trust again, she realized. But looking straight into the crystal-clear depths of his eyes, Ronnie's fears had melted. Along with her heart.

She groaned. Another cliché. But true.

When she drove back, Ronnie was disappointed to see that Red's truck wasn't in the driveway. What was keeping him? She went to check on Ginger and let her out of the carrier for a few minutes. Her footsteps slowed as she heard Casson mentioning Red's name.

He must have called…

"He said he had made a mistake, and he should have never started up with her. He said he couldn't face her…" Casson's voice drifted off.

Ronnie had heard enough. She back-tracked quietly up the stairs and into the guest bathroom. She sat on the edge of the tub and stared numbly at the opposite wall. *He wasn't coming.* She felt as if a slab of ice had rammed into her stomach. He had seemed so genuine earlier. She had believed his words, felt the passion of his kisses. How could he have suddenly changed his mind about her? About them? Yes, he'd been hurt. So had she. But she had been ready to let him into her life, and she had believed that he had felt the same about her. Tears of shock and frustration spilled onto her cheeks.

Maybe reality had hit him square in the jaw, the reality that by wanting Ronnie, he'd be getting a two-for-one deal. And maybe that had scared him enough to make him back off. She frowned, mentally playing the reel of what he had said to her in the truck. He couldn't forget her. He had fallen head over heels for her…

Ronnie's heart froze. He hadn't once mentioned Andy.

And she had been too caught up with the fantasy of Red loving her—

But no, he hadn't used the word "love" either.

Ronnie's stomach vaulted. How could she trust and have faith in someone who wasn't ready to accept her child? No matter how attracted she was to Red physically, there could be no going forward if he couldn't see himself including Andy in the picture.

This was a bad dream. She would wake up and see Red walking into the house, his eyes twinkling. Reflecting his love. And trust. And desire to get to know and love Andy.

Ronnie walked to the window and looked out. No truck. It wasn't a dream.

The chunk of ice that had struck her in the stomach now seemed like it was breaking off into icicles down her limbs. Casson's voice came back to her: *he said he couldn't face her...*

Her heart twisted. Red had ruined everything. Her day, her hopes and her dreams. He had destroyed her trust. *She* should have never started up with *him*.

Ronnie was done with trusting men.

And she never wanted to see Red's face again.

She dabbed at her eyes. She had Andy to

think about now. Her beautiful, courageous little boy. And she was not about to ruin his birthday. She checked her watch. With a leaden heart, she opened the door and went downstairs.

Red looked at the endless lines of backed-up traffic ahead of him and behind. He had just passed Barrie and like a thousand other vehicles, he was stuck in a traffic jam on the 400 North. He rubbed his temples, then glanced at his watch. Damn. He had been so happy, getting to Toronto fairly quickly, grabbing the jersey and hockey stick in his new penthouse and wrapping them up before immediately heading back to Parry Sound. From his memory of a photo of Andy at Casson's house, and his photo in the locket Ronnie had shown him, Red kept picturing Andy's face lighting up at seeing Ginger and the hockey gifts.

When he finally pulled into Winter's Haven, he was relieved to see Ronnie's car still there.

The shocked look on Ronnie's face when she opened the door made him frown. Something had happened. "Is Andy okay?" he said, reaching to clasp her hand.

Ronnie pulled her hand away. "He's fine,"

she said woodenly. "I wasn't thinking of my son earlier," she said stiffly. "I made a mistake. Just like you."

"I don't understand, Ronnie." Red stared at the woman standing across from him, a look of aloofness and disdain on her face. He felt as if he had just stepped into a twilight zone.

"Just go," she snapped before turning away.

CHAPTER TWENTY-FOUR

RONNIE STARED AT JUSTINE. "What did you say?"

"Casson had been filling me in on what had happened with Red and his previous girl-friend. And her son, Marco."

Ronnie blinked, stunned. She had gone to find Justine and had burst into tears in the baby's room as she explained what had happened.

"I really messed up, didn't I?" Ronnie wiped her eyes. "I treated him like…like dirt down there."

At the sudden rumble outside, Ronnie rushed to the window. Red was putting on his seat belt.

She flew down the stairs, slipped on her boots, but didn't bother with her coat. She rushed out the door and down the steps, only to catch a glimpse of Red's back bumper before it disappeared.

Ronnie's heart plummeted. She turned and began to walk slowly toward the house.

A crunching noise in the driveway made her look back. Her heart began to clang. Red was driving back. She couldn't move. The truck came to a stop and Red jumped out. He took one look at Ronnie and gathered her in his arms. "Get in," he said huskily.

He helped her up, closed the door and got back in. He handed her some tissues, and after she had dabbed at her eyes, he took her hands in his. "Okay, Forrester, let it out. All of it."

She couldn't stop shivering. He took off his jacket and put it over her shoulders. "I'm listening," he murmured.

His gentle tone was enough to cause another round of sobbing. When her tears had subsided, she explained what had happened, how she had misinterpreted the conversation she had overheard. "I was so mean, turning into an ice queen and ordering you to leave."

"I'm pretty sure I can melt your icy heart," he murmured, before explaining why he had been late.

"You went all the way to Toronto to get those gifts for Andy?"

"I did."

Something flickered in his eyes, and Ronnie felt her heart tumbling in her chest. If she hadn't expressed it before, she had to tell him now. "I love you, Red Brannigan II." She cupped his face. "Do you hear me?"

"Loud and clear, Ronnie Forrester. And I love you more." He grinned before leaning forward to kiss her deeply.

"I can't exactly get down on my knee in this truck," he murmured in her ear, "but I plan to do so very soon in a more comfortable place. In the meantime, could I have the honor of attending Andy's birthday, and accompanying both of you to the grand opening of Franklin's Resort next week?"

"I'll say yes, but you'll have to run it by the little guy too."

He chuckled. "I think I can handle that. Now how about we go back inside so I can meet the birthday boy and watch him open his presents. And have some cake, of course." His eyes glittered. "Although I plan to drop by your place later...*much later*...for some real dessert."

Ronnie felt her heart skip a beat. Oh, yes. That was exactly the dessert she had in mind.

Red suggested that Ronnie go in the house first, while he grabbed the presents for Andy. He felt excited and a little nervous at the same time. What if Andy took a disliking to him? What if he didn't want to share his mom with anybody else? The poor kid had already dealt with his dad leaving him for a period of time; would he be wary of another man coming into his life?

Red knocked on the door, and when Ronnie opened it moments later, his pulse leaped. He searched her face, wondering if there was any sign of regret at having him come to Andy's birthday, but all he saw was a shy smile and luminous eyes with lashes that fluttered with restrained excitement.

"Hi," he said huskily. "Have you cleared my entry with the boss?" He waved over her head to Casson and Justine, who had entered the kitchen.

"Don't kid yourself," Casson replied with a laugh. "Ronnie's her own boss."

"I actually meant Andy," Red said with a smile.

"Oh, that boss. He's in the living room, playing with our dog, Luna." He checked his watch. "I think we can head there now and get this party started." He took the packages from Red.

Red followed them all into the living room, thinking about how just mentioning Andy's name had felt as if the child were already in his life... He watched Casson zigzagging around Andy and Luna before placing the two parcels in a corner with the other presents. When Andy noticed the packages, he came to a sudden stop and Luna careened into him, knocking him off balance.

Red swooped forward in a rush of adrenaline and caught the boy before he went crashing to the floor and ended up with a concussion. For several moments time stood still. Andy blinked at him with a mixture of surprise and curiosity in his dark eyes. Everyone else in the room faded from Red's view, even though they were just steps away, leaving the next few seconds to play out in slow motion...

The boy's hair was tousled, and his plaid shirt had flopped out of his pants. His cheeks were flushed, and his eyes—Ronnie's eyes—brought a lump to Red's throat, in addition to igniting an accelerating drum beat in his chest. The kid was so vulnerable. No wonder Ronnie was such a protective parent.

And he could be, too... He was ready...

Red knew in that instant that he would love this little imp as if he were his own...and maybe one day in the future, he and Ronnie could give him a special gift of a baby brother or sister...

He wished he could hug Andy right this

minute, and tell him that he'd be there to catch him in the years ahead but that moment would have to wait.

As Red set him down, everyone came back into focus. Red's gaze flew to Ronnie, and he knew immediately that she had been touched by these past moments too...

"Thanks, mister." Andy's voice brought his attention back to the boy, who was stretching his neck to the max to talk to him.

He smiled and crouched down so he could be at eye level with Andy. "No problem. And you can call me Red."

"Red?" Andy's gaze flew to Red's hair.

Red chuckled. "Well, my mother couldn't exactly call me Purple with hair like this, could she?"

Andy giggled. "No." He suddenly turned and scampered off to the corner with the pile of presents. "Can I open my presents, Mummy?"

Ronnie walked across the room, squeezing Red's hand slightly before joining Andy. "I guess we can switch the order of things," she said, ruffling Andy's hair. "Presents, then lunch, then cake. How does that sound?"

"Yay! That sounds great!" Andy clapped vigorously, and Luna bounded toward him, her tail wagging.

* * *

Andy had opened up Casson and Justine's gift—a high-powered telescope and an astronomy book for kids—hugged them both, and was now eyeing Red's gifts. Red handed the smaller gift to him with the Toronto Maple Leafs hockey jersey first, and smiled when Andy opened it and cheered. And although the shape of the next gift had made it pretty obvious, Andy jumped up and down when he saw all the signatures on the hockey stick.

"Okay, sweetie, put it down now before someone loses their head," Ronnie said firmly. "Your next gift is upstairs. Close your eyes and count to twenty while I go and get it."

Moments later, Ronnie returned with the carrier concealed under a box that had holes cut out strategically in it. "Okay, Andy, at the count of three, you can open your eyes and lift the box." She set the box down in front of him. "One, two, three. Okay, lift...and meet Ginger!"

Andy's eyes grew wide. "Mummy, Mummy, you got me a kitten!" He threw his arms around her neck. "Thanks, Mummy!"

Red was glad that Casson had been taking photos with his cell phone. These were memories that Ronnie would cherish forever.

Seeing her gaze at Andy with such love made his heart ache with love for her.

At the sudden cry coming from the baby monitor, Justine went upstairs to check on A.J. Casson followed, with Luna bolting after him.

Ronnie let Ginger out of the carrier. Andy picked her up right away and kissed her before walking over to Red, who stroked the kitten's back, smiling at the memories he already had of her. Ronnie sat next to Red on the couch and watched with an indulgent grin on her face.

Andy was a lucky kid to have Ronnie as a mother. And she was lucky to have *him*.

Here was a little guy who had gone through an ordeal no kid—or parent—should have to go through, and had finished his treatment with positive results. Results worth celebrating. No wonder Ronnie had wanted to get Andy something superspecial for his birthday.

"Her fur is the color of your hair, Red. It's so nice," Andy said, making the back of Red's eyes suddenly start to prickle.

His heart swelled. This was what he had always dreamed of, sharing special moments… with his family.

EPILOGUE

ALONG WITH THE thrum of the helicopter's engines, Ronnie felt a warm thrum in her chest. Andy was sitting next to her, and Red was in the seat directly across from them. They were all wearing protective headsets, and Andy looked so small in his. Her eyes began to mist. This was a dream she had never envisioned, flying over Toronto at night, viewing the jeweled skyline and multicolored beams of light from the skyscrapers reflected in the shimmering waters of Lake Ontario.

And sitting across from the helicopter's owner, Redmond Brannigan II.

In the couple of weeks since Andy's birthday party, Ronnie had felt like she was on top of the clouds. Red had taken her and Andy for an extensive tour of his Victorian mansion, and Andy had been delighted with the secret nooks and crannies, and the hidden staircase up to the attic. Red had shown him and Ronnie the designed templates on his laptop for the pool and water slide, basketball court, treehouse, and mini movie theater, and Andy had looked at him with big brown eyes and said eagerly, "Can we come and visit you when they're done?"

Red had exchanged a smile with Ronnie, a smile that had filled her with such emotion that she had had to discreetly blot the tears that were starting to blur her vision. She and Red had agreed that they would let Andy get used to the idea of them being friends and sharing some good times together before letting him know that they would be sharing the rest of their lives together as a family...

Casson and Justine had invited them all to their place for skating on the frozen stretch of bay, and then later, dinner and a bonfire, roasting marshmallows and drinking hot chocolate. Red had taken turns with Ronnie skating alongside Andy, and at one point, Red had asked Andy if he was up to speed skating—which meant being carried as Red speed skated. Andy had said yes and Ronnie had watched with a thumping heart as Red zoomed around the ice, with Andy's little arms around his neck and his face registering both excitement and joy.

Ronnie's heart had done a pole vault a couple of days later when Andy had asked Ronnie if Red could come over to help them make peanut butter cookies. "He's funny," he had said matter-of-factly to Ronnie, "and he said he would help me build something awesome with my LEGO set."

Later that evening, watching them both on the living room floor, working together with the colored blocks, Ronnie had taken the tray of cookies that Andy and Red had made out of the oven. She had noticed that R+R+A had been etched into one of them and had looked up quickly to find Red's gaze fixed on her. And then he had winked.

Yes, she had been floating on top of the clouds...

And now she almost *was*, soaring in Red's helicopter over Toronto.

Red had reminded her of their conversation about returning to the city for a night view. Ronnie had thought to herself that returning alone would be bittersweet, like taking in a star-studded sky alone, without anyone to share the magic of it.

Well, she had returned with the man who had put stars in her eyes, and it felt so, so sweet. Last night, Red had told her to clear her schedule for midafternoon; he had a surprise for her and Andy. The only instructions he had given her were to go to Casson and Justine's place and to look out the big bay window at 4:00 p.m. She and Andy had done so, with Casson and Justine looking on, and at precisely 4:00 p.m., they heard an approaching rumble. Andy had let out a squeal when the blue-and-white helicopter had come into view and not long afterward, started to descend, whirling to a stop on the frozen bay, yards away from the skating surface.

Red had emerged wearing his headset, and carrying a bag. He glided across the ice and minutes later was in the house, inviting Ronnie and Andy to go for a ride in his helicopter, and handing them their headsets. Ronnie had caught the gleam in Casson's and Justine's eyes as she and Andy had gotten dressed. "You knew about this," she accused them, and they laughed and waved her off.

The pilot had greeted them and, after they were all safely secured in their seats, started the engines. Andy had been mesmerized the whole time as they flew past Parry Sound and the Thirty Thousand Islands along Georgian Bay, and over the Muskokas. The vast wooded areas looked like an enchanted wonderland with their snow-dusted boughs sparkling in the sun along countless lakes. Sitting next to her, Andy was practically glued to the windowpane, and when they reached Toronto and the CN Tower came into view, he cried out, "Look, Mummy! Look!"

Ronnie was in awe herself, and despite her initial worry that she would become light-headed or queasy as she had been on Red's penthouse terrace, she had experienced none of those symptoms so far.

Red had intermittently pointed out buildings that Brannigan Architects International had been commissioned to design, and when he indicated the Four-Leaf Clover, the residence tower with his penthouse, he told Ronnie that he had been the one to design it. When she looked up at him in awe, the gleam in his eyes as his gaze dropped to her lips made her pulse quicken.

He, too, was thinking of the kiss they had exchanged there...

When daylight turned to dusk, the pilot circled back toward the entertainment district. Looking out the window to the dazzling lights of the city against a backdrop of apricot and red-orange sky blotted with indigo clouds took Ronnie's breath away. The multicolored lights emanating from the skyscrapers were reflected in shimmering beams in the dark waters by the Harbourfront. The alternating lights of the CN Tower, both on 360 and along the length of the tower, made her catch her breath with their flashes of red and yellow, purple and electric blue.

"I love the pulsating energy of the city," he said, leaning forward, "but I also love the quiet and tranquility of Parry Sound." His eyes probed hers. "Do you think you can handle being a country *and* a city girl? I want to make some new memories with you and Andy in Toronto."

Ronnie swallowed a lump in her throat. She sensed that Red was referring to the time she and Andy had spent here in hospital. When they had passed over the downtown core, Ronnie had felt a momentary sadness, peering down at the cluster of hospitals that included SickKids. And then she was overwhelmed with a feeling of gratitude for everyone there who had helped her little boy... like guardian angels.

"I think I can handle it," she said breathlessly. Parry Sound was only a couple of hours away from Toronto.

"Good. No, *great*!" He squeezed her hands and brought them up to kiss them. "We'll enjoy the best of both worlds..." He glanced at Andy, who was still scrunched up against the window.

Suddenly Red looked at Ronnie's left hand and frowned.

"What's the matter?" Ronnie stared down at her hand.

Without letting go of her hand, Red unbuckled his seat belt, slid off his seat and knelt on one knee. He reached in the back pocket of his jeans and pulled out a small black velvet box. "Something's missing on your hand, that's the matter…" he said huskily.

Ronnie's heart stopped for a moment and then began pulsing at the sight of the large marquise-shaped diamond nestled inside. She blinked up at Red and back down at the platinum ring that he now held in his fingers.

"You are the jewel in my life, Ronnie."

Her head snapped back up and she realized that Andy had turned to look at them with interest.

"This ring doesn't compare in value to *you*, Ronnie," he said, his eyes bright. "I offer it to you with my promise to love you and your little squirt over there for the rest of my days. To cherish our family, and to always be there for you both. And for any little carrottop or rabbit that might join us in the future… Veronica Forrester, will you—"

"Yes! I will, Red Brannigan II!" She took

a deep breath as he slid the ring on her finger, and thought her heart would burst when Andy started clapping.

"I'll take that as a sign of approval," Red laughed, before kissing her soundly. He gazed at her hand. "I hope you like it."

"It's beautiful," she told him. "I want to pick out a special ring for you, too, Red, but for now—" she shrugged and gave him a teasing smile "—all I can offer you is a plate of peanut butter cookies when we get back to the cottage."

"Mmm... Deal!" He stood up and turned to Andy, raising his hand, and Ronnie's heart swelled as the two loves of her life gave each other a high five.

* * * * *

If you enjoyed this story,
check out these other great reads from
Rosanna Battigelli

Caribbean Escape with the Tycoon
Captivated by Her Italian Boss
Swept Away by the Enigmatic Tycoon

All available now!